Jessica Watkins Presents

A BATON ROUGE LOVE STORY
Loving You Through The Pain

by **JOHNAZIA GRAY**

Chapter One

Purity sat on her bed Indian-style with tears spilling down her cheeks. Even the loud music coming through the headphones over her ears couldn't block out her mother, Tawny's, verbal abuse. It was almost like her mother ruined the days that she enjoyed the most.

"You think you're better than me, but that's cool. You won't be shit in life if you keep that attitude up, little bitch," Tawny argued.

Purity could never understand how her mother allowed money to be the reason why she treated her so badly. Tawny's own mother, Aretha, had died two years ago and left Tawny *nothing*, but she left Purity and Tawny's sister,everything. Aretha was a God-fearing woman, and she followed the Bible's teachings. Tawny was ruined because she'd been raped when she was a child by her stepfather, and she had

1

hatred in her heart ever since then. Even though her mother had almost killed her husband behind the incident and then divorced him, Tawny was still mean and evil toward Aretha. Aretha was a hard-working woman who cleaned houses and buildings for a living. She wasn't rich, but she met some amazing people who always looked out for her and her daughters. Tawny always said how her mother was a disgrace because she cleaned for white people and didn't get a regular job like everyone else. Tawny was so mean that she ran her sister, Chrystal, from the house when she was just seventeen. She couldn't take the mistreatment and harshness that her older sister dished out. When Aretha passed away from a heart attack, she left Purity everything that she had: the house that she owned and the fifty-five thousand dollars that was given to her as a gift from her friends. She even left her the bike that she used to get back and forth to work with.

Purity's whole world came crashing down when her grandmother died. Because of her grandmother,

Purity wasn't evil like her mom. She was loving, caring, and sweet. Aretha cherished Purity because Tawny was never there for her while she was coming up. She left all the motherly duties to Aretha and because of that, Purity looked at her grandmother as the mother, and her mother as a sister. She called her grandmother *Ma,* while she called Tawny by her name. Even though she called her mother by her name she still respected her like she was the best mother in the world.

"Retha ain't give a shit about neither of us, Purity. That's why she let that man do that shit to me when I was little. If he was around, she would've done the same thing to you," she yelled.

"That's not true! Ma loved me, and she loved you too! You're just evil, Tawny!" Purity yelled.

Tawny was taken aback because Purity never raised her voice. Purity should've never let her know that she got under her skin.

"Your ass is evil. I asked you for five hundred little-ass dollars, and you're complaining. Retha left you all that money, and all you do is pay the bills and put food in the house. You can't look out for me?"

Fed up, Purity yelled, "You're grown, Tawny. Ma told me to take care of this house, and that's what I'm doing. I don't use the money for nonsense. I get up every day and *work*. You can do it too if you really wanted too. You're just lazy."

Tawny walked up and pointed in Purity's face. "Who the fuck you think you talking too, *bitch?*"

Purity couldn't take it anymore. She hopped off of the bed and pushed Tawny into the wall by her head. Because Tawny was stronger and a more experienced in fighter, she was able to get the best of Purity.

"You gon' hit me, bitch?" Tawny punched Purity in the eye.

"Ahhhhh!" Purity screamed out in frustration. She grabbed Tawny by her long, thick hair, pulling it from the roots. She kicked Tawny in the knee causing her to fall to the floor and she began to pound her in the head.

"*You're evil!*" Purity screamed and cried. Tawny couldn't get up because of the position Purity had her in. Her wild hair blocked her vision, and she couldn't see.

"Let go of my fucking hair!" Tawny yelled.

Purity mushed her head and took a few steps back. With a busted lip, and a swollen eye she stood over her mother and shook her head."I can't take this anymore! I'm leaving!" she yelled.

"No, you stay here and pay all these bills. I'll leave. I don't need this shit. Fuck you and Aretha. She raised your ass to look down on me, but always remember with that attitude you have you will always fail."

Purity's mouth dropped open. Before she knew it, they were throwing blows again. But this time Purity was fucking Tawny up. She punched Tawny so hard in the nose that she knew that it was broken. She slung Tawny all across the room and pounded her in her head.

"You gon' say that 'bout Ma?" She pushed her head into the floor. "You stupid, bitch! I'll kill you in this house, Tawny."

"Man, what the fuck? Chill out, Purity." Her older cousin, Tarvis, broke the two women up. He came at the right time because the two of them were about to kill each other.

"Why the fuck are y'all in here fighting? What's up?" Tarvis held Purity in his arms.

"Get off of me, Tarvis! Just get off of me!"

Tawny rested on Purity's bed and tasted the blood from her busted mouth. She couldn't believe that Purity had finally grown the balls to fight back. After jumping on her, and cursing her out all of her life, Purity couldn't take the shit anymore. She didn't deserve it. She was a twenty-one-year-old naïve girl who went to school fulltime at Baton Rouge School of Court Reporting, she worked at the courthouse, and she wasn't in the streets unlike some of the girls around the way. The only thing that kept Purity there in that house with her mother was Aretha. Before she died, she made Purity promise that she wouldn't give up on her mother. Because she loved her grandmother so much, she had promised, but Purity couldn't understand how her grandma had dealt with that shit all of those years. She understood why her auntie had left the house at an early age. That crazy bitch would drive anyone insane.

"You brought my weed?" Tawny asked Tarvis.

Tarvis was Chrystal's oldest son. He and his auntie would smoke a few blunts together and she would buy her weed from him. Tarvis always told Tawny how she should've had boys instead of girls due to her being so tough.

"Here, man." He threw the sack of weed in her hand. "I'ma take Purity over here to Mama's house."

Purity stuffed her overnight bag with a lot of outfits. She needed to get away from there for a few days, and her auntie's house would be the perfect place to be. She grabbed her books, laptop, phone, and followed her big cousin out the door. She sat in the passenger's seat and breathed heavily from the anger she had built up inside of her.

"Finally tired, huh?" Tarvis asked as he pulled out of the driveway.

"*I'm sick of this shit!*" Purity yelled. She was beyond frustrated.

Tarvis didn't say much, he just drove and allowed her to vent. He knew that sooner or later that she and her mother would have a big brawl because Purity was always too nice and patient with Tawny. Tarvis also knew that his little cousin was a good girl and that she didn't deserve to be mistreated by her mother.

"I don't know what the fuck she wants from me. I'm twenty-one years old. I have no fucking kids and I'm a virgin. I don't do shit but go to work and school. I live my fucking life like a teenager, and she still treats me like I'm the worst child ever. I'm supposed to be happy, man." She wiped her tears and continued. "Life wasn't this bad when Ma was living, man." She shook her head.

"I feel you, cuz. That shit that Tawny be on is crazy, but whether you believe it or not she loves you. She's just fucked up in the head."

"She don't love me. She's the reason my self-esteem is so fucking low. She tries to make me believe that I'm not pretty. She's so harsh. I'm over her."

Tarvis shook his head. "Girl, you're beautiful as fuck. Don't you ever question that."

"So, why don't I have a boyfriend? I've never been asked out on a date. Everything she says to me is true. Don't nobody want my ass."

"What you want a nigga to do? Break in the house and find you? For one, you're bitter because that's what you're allowing yourself to be. Did you hear what you just said to me? You don't do shit but go to school and work. Your life is gonna pass you by like that, Ma. That's why Vanity and Vix are always trying to get you out of the house. You need to live a little bit, and as far as you being a virgin is concerned, keep it that way. Ain' no nigga worth giving up the pussy to these days, and that's real."

The things that Tarvis had said gave her something to think about. He was right. How was she going to be happy if she didn't live her life? Tarvis' sisters, Vanity and Vix, always tried to get Purity out of the house simply because she was a beautiful, miserable, lost little girl. Vanity was twenty-four, and Vix was twenty-six. Vix was married to Baton Rouge's biggest kingpin, Paul, and they had two kids together. Even though Vix was the oldest and had the perfect family, she still lived her life. Vanity, on the other hand, was young, wild, and free, which was something that Purity had told herself that she would *never* be. Vanity could be your bitch today and somebody else's bitch the next day. She wasn't tying herself down to nobody.

"Maybe I should start hanging with Vanity and Vix, huh?"

"Man, those two right there are hell, but they'll teach you a few things."

They both laughed.

"I need to start somewhere, man. But first things first…I have to move from that house. Seriously. I'll pay the bills and everything, but that's it for me. I can't stay there. It's not even the same with Ma being gone anyway."

Tarvis shrugged his shoulders, "Do what's best for you, baby girl. You deserve it."

When they pulled up to Chrystal's house, the two of them got out of the car and walked inside. Vix's two little boys were sitting at the dinner table saying their grace while Chrystal stood at the island fixing a plate of spaghetti and salad.

Chrystal hugged Purity. "Hey, my baby, what brought you over here so late?"

"Me and Tawny got into a big fight tonight, Auntie." She lowered her head.

"*What?*" Chrystal yelled.

"She ain't lying, Mama. I had to break them up," Tarvis said, fixing a plate of food.

"Purity," Chrystal dragged, "You know better than to fight your mama girl. Ma ain't raise you like that."

Purity eyes watered and she shook her head. "I know, Auntie. Ma's probably rolling over in her grave. But Tawny was being so nasty. She said fuck me *and* Mama. I flipped."

Chrystal shook her head. Nothing her niece had told her was new to her. That's what type of person Tawny was. It was sad that after all the years that had passed by she was still the same. Chrystal was glad that she was right with the Lord. She refused to have all those demons around her like her big sister had.

"Lord Jesus... All I can do is pray for my sister. What was she arguing about this time?"

"She wanted me to give her five hundred dollars out of the money M left me, and I wouldn't."

"Five hundred damn dollars for what?" Chrystal asked.

"Who knows? Probably to take care of one of her niggas." Purity rolled her eyes.

"Tawny needs to find a job and get over herself. She know that's *your* money that Mama left you."

"But I still don't touch that money unless it's for the bills around the house and things we need, Auntie. I don't just spend that money. I work every day just so I can have my own spending money. Tawny should do the same thing."

Chrystal chuckled and shook her head. Her poor niece was such a good girl. She wished like hell that her two daughters could be like her. "Baby, Mama left you that money to help you to live a comfortable life; not to just pay those bills. Stop using that as an excuse. You don't have to give Tawny shit. She's a grown-ass woman. She didn't deserve that money because she treated Mama like a dog. Spend your money how you want to."

Purity smiled at her auntie. "Maybe I should do what you did."

Aside from the money that Aretha had left Purity, she'd left Chrystal every single dime that she had in her savings account. Aretha's oldest son,

Keldrick, was sent to prison for fifteen years and was beaten to death by on-duty officers. After his death, Aretha sued the Mississippi Department of Corrections and walked away with half a million dollars. Of course Aretha, being the woman that she was, never touched the money. She told everyone that she was saving it for hard times, knowing that she had already designated in her will that her daughter, Chrystal, would receive the money.

Chrystal was humble like her mother, so she didn't do the most. She stayed in a comfortable five bedroom, three bathroom home that she had built from the ground. It was beyond nice, but it was simple and just enough for her family. She also had her own drug store right across the tracks in the hood, and she drove a 2016 Toyota Camry SE. She was happy with herself and her life. She had three amazing kids, two grandchildren, and she was married to her high school sweetheart. Purity looked up to her auntie, and she wanted to be exactly like her someday.

"You have to start somewhere," her auntie said and smiled. "But get that phone over there and call your mother and apologize first."

"Nope." Purity stood to her feet. "Not tonight, Auntie. That lady has done it for real this time. Give me a minute to pray and talk to the Lord before I call her."

Chrystal chuckled. "I understand."

"I'ma go in here and get myself prepared for bed. When Vix comes to pick up the boys, can you tell her to stop by the room? I need some hangout partners."

"Lord, have mercy, Jesus." She nodded. "Yeah, I'll tell her."

Purity kissed her aunt on the cheek and walked to the back of the house.

Chapter Two

After grabbing her briefcase, MacBook, and purse, Purity stepped down from her desk and left the courtroom. Being a court reporter wasn't the easiest job, but she enjoyed doing it because it was her passion. Surprisingly, the case docket for that day wasn't very hectic, which wasn't normal for a Friday. Purity made good money being a court reporter, and she was one of the best that some of the judges ever had. She took her job very seriously, and because of that, she been offered many different employment opportunities outside of the courtroom.

She walked into the bathroom and took off her tan and gold, suede Michael Kors four-inch heels. She hated walking in heels, but she had to keep up with the professional girly look as her auntie had told her to. She switched into some comfortable sandals and let her long hair down from the ponytail and ran her hand through her thick, bushy bang. She smiled and winked at herself.

She walked out of the bathroom toward the exit. Because she was so focused on her phone and her Facebook notifications, she wasn't paying attention to where she was going. She bumped into someone, knocking her entire computer out of her hand and onto the floor.

"Shit," she mumbled as she looked at the beautiful computer that was now damaged. "I am so sorry." She apologized to the guy she bumped into.

When she looked up and noticed that it was Paul, her cousin, Vix's husband, she smiled.

"Paul, look what you made me do," she pouted.

"I didn't make you do shit, P. You bumped into me." After helping her pick up the broken pieces to her computer he held it in his hand and then hugged her. "Damn, P. I can buy you another one if you need me to. You fucked it up."

"As much as I want to scream, I'm not even going to allow it to ruin my day."

Purity's eyes were on the handsome man standing behind Paul. He was about six-one in height and his muscles stuck out so lovely. His arms were covered in tattoos which only made him look even better. What took the cake was his smooth, glistening caramel skin and his freshly lined beard. Even the little scar above his forehead was cute. Nothing was wrong about that nigga. *This nigga even got the waves,* Purity thought. She couldn't believe that he was dressed in a suit. But the suit meant nothing, though because if he was hanging out with Paul, Purity knew he wasn't the one for her.

"What are you doing up here at courthouse anyway, big head?" She asked, turning her attention back to Paul.

"Had to handle some shit with my brother."

"Your brother?" she asked with her eyes widened. "Your *real* brother?"

"That nigga don't look like me to you?" Paul asked, making the guy smile,showing off his beautiful teeth.

Purity smiled and nodded her head. "Damn, he actually does. I didn't know you had a brother, though."

"Yeah, well, I didn't either, but we'll talk about that later. Vix told me that you were going out with us tonight."

"Yes, I am. I'm excited. Can you believe it?"

"No, I actually can't."

They shared a laugh.

"Well, I guess I'll see you later tonight, cousin-in-law. Thanks for breaking my new computer," she said, walking away.

"Don't tell your cousin I did that!"

"I won't." Purity laughed.

Carstin watched Purity as she walked towards the exit. He looked at his brother and said "I got to have her, man."

Paul chuckled and gave him a quick rundown on how Purity was.

Paul and Carstin had only known that they were blood brothers for two months, and they were already inseparable. The only thing that brought them together was their father's death. Neither of them was hurt because he was a deadbeat-ass nigga. When Paul found out that he had a little brother, he was excited and couldn't give up the chance on getting to know him. The guys' mothers didn't even know that the other existed. That's how terrible of a father Paul Senior was. Everyone was even surprised that the sperm donor had even included his two sons in his million-dollar will. Paul and Carstin were to split the money down the middle. Paul Senior was married to Sarah Paden, one of the richest white women in Baton Rouge, Louisiana. She instantly became his meal ticket once they became husband and wife.

Sarah's great grandparents were slave masters back in the day and owned land and other different properties all over Baton Rouge and surrounding areas. Leaving everyone in her family a nice loop. Every generation in their family cherished all the land and properties that their grandparents owned but after Sarah's parents passed away, she sold all of the land she'd inherited and made millions. Because she was so in love with Paul, she made sure he owned half of everything she'd inherited. The only thing Paul had to do to keep her happy was hide his kids from her family and pretend that they did not exist. He could only acknowledge his daughter and son that Sarah had birthed. He didn't give a damn that he was a disgrace to his family and others at the time. He had money and that's all that mattered to him. When he found out that he only had a few weeks to live from cancer it caused him to turn to God and ask for forgiveness. He reached out to Paul Junior several times, asking him to come and visit him before he died, but he never did. When he decided to reach out to Carstin, it was too late. Because he felt guilty for how he turned his back on his children he left them all of his money.

Paul Junior used to always call his daddy a house nigga, but as prideful as he was, he didn't reject the money that Paul Senior left him, and neither did Carstin. The two unacknowledged sons had their own money without the inheritance of their father, but his money made their lives better.

The two brothers had learned each other in a short period of time, which was perfect. Even though Carstin was originally from Jackson, Mississippi, he knew that God had placed his brother in his life at a certain time for a reason because he was ready to relocate. And Baton Rouge seemed to be a great place to be. Everyone seemed down to earth and cool, and he really didn't have anyone back home besides his mother and stepfather.

Purity exited the building and hopped into her 2015 Chrysler 200 and drove to the Mall of Louisiana to find her something nice to wear to the club. She was excited that she was finally about to step out of her comfort zone and have a good time with her cousins. She needed the adventure, and she hoped and prayed that it would be a night to remember.

Her phone rang, and she rolled her eyes to the top of her head when she saw Tawny's picture pop up on the caller ID. Instead of ignoring the call, she answered respectfully, "Yes, ma'am?"

"Did you pay the light and water bill today?" she asked sadly.

"Of course I did. Why wouldn't I?"

Feeling relieved she began her verbal abuse. "I thought you were probably gonna be a bitch and leave the bills to me."

Aggravated, Purity responded, "Tawny, I paid the bills for the entire month and you know that. If you called to verbally assault me, I'm about to hang up the phone."

"Girl, what the fuck ever. As long as you paid the bills, that's all I care about. When are you coming back home?"

"I should be there in a few days to get the rest of my stuff and move it to storage."

"*What?!*" she yelled.

"Yeah…" Purity smirked as if Tawny could see her.

"Aretha has to be rolling over in her grave right now. Her ol' precious jewel is leaving her house behind."

Purity sighed. "I have to go." She hung up the phone. She wanted to sit in the car and cry as she normally would, but she was tired of allowing Tawny to have control over her life. She now understood that her mother had only picked on her all these years because she'd allowed her to. But that was all over now.

After spending hours in the mall Purity was satisfied that she had found something grown and sexy to wear. She'd purchased a pair of heels from Aldo and a simple, but beautiful dress from Forever 21. She realized she was a little cheap and didn't go all the way out like Vanity and Vix did, but she enjoyed being responsible with her money. She grabbed a meal from the food court and headed to her auntie's house to relax before she got her night started. When she pulled into the driveway, she was thankful that no one was home from work because she wanted the quiet time.

Chapter Three

"I'm asking, though, is little Mama gonna be there for real?" Carstin asked his big brother, Paul.

"You heard what she said, nigga. Leave her alone, though. She's a good one."

"I'm a good one too, shit." Carstin giggled.

The very first moment Carstin laid eyes on her in that courtroom he knew he had to get at her some type of way. She was beautiful to him. So beautiful he barely even got the time to check out her body. He was so infatuated with her beautiful smile, her squeaky voice, and her pretty skin. If he could've rubbed his hands over her face and caressed her right there in the courthouse, he would've been grateful. He was so ready to see her at the club.

"I got a meeting in an hour. You going with me?" Paul asked, pouring himself a glass of green apple Crown Royal.

"Yeah, I'm there." Carstin lit his blunt and laid back on the comfortable sofa.

Paul and Carstin kicked it in his man cave every day. Paul had to admit that he had been in his man cave more since Carstin had been there, but he wasn't tripping. Building a bond with his little brother meant way more than being in the streets.

Vix walked in, interrupting them. "Hey, babe. Dinner is ready if y'all are hungry."

"We ain't hungry, baby."

Vix sighed. "You sure, babe? I cooked a big-ass dinner just for you and Carstin."

Carstin smiled. "I'll take some, sis."

"You're way sweeter than your brother," Vixen said, returning the smile before she walked away.

Paul shook his head. Loving Vix was one hell of a job. Even though she hadn't been the most faithful wife that she was supposed to be, he still loved her unconditionally because he was the cause of it.

Carstin passed the blunt to Paul. "You got a good woman, bruh."

He nodded his head. "Yeah, that's my shawty."

Carstin's phone continuously rang, but he hit ignore repeatedly.

"Damn, nigga. You ain't gon' answer that?"

He waved his hand in the air. "That's just a bitch begging for some dick. I ain't thinking about her ass."

"I know how that goes!" Paul nodded his head.

"I know you fucking do, asshole!" Vix shoved the plate that he told her he didn't want to him.

"I didn't even hear you walk in here," Paul explained.

"It don't make a fucking difference, nigga. I still heard your dumb ass." She argued. After handing Carstin his plate, she stormed out and headed back upstairs.

Paul became quiet. He knew not to argue with Vix.

In the beginning of their marriage, Paul went to prison for a year and a day. While he was locked up, Vix got a phone call from a woman claiming that she was pregnant with Paul's child. The only reason why Vix believed what the lady had told her was because Paul had taken the woman on a trip to Jamaica and she had pictures to prove it. Vix stop riding for him and had a little fun while he was away. She got pregnant by another kingpin named Hazel, but of course she got rid of the baby. She had vowed to never have a baby if it wasn't from her husband. The both of them did some things in their marriage that they regretted, but they had put too much time and effort into their relationship to settle for a divorce. Having kids together made it even harder to walk away. Even though Paul never had it, the both of them believed in a two-parent home.

Carstin laughed. "Go fuck her good, and she'll get over it."

"I know my wife, little nigga."

Carstin finished his food and stood to his feet. "Where's your meeting at this time?" he asked.

"Same place. You might as well ride with me. It won't be long today, though because we're turning the fuck up tonight."

Carstin nodded his head and grabbed his phone to return a few phone calls while Paul headed upstairs to find his wife. He quietly walked into the master bedroom only to find his beautiful, thick, scrumptious wife applying makeup to her beautiful face. She ignored his presence and applied some red berry lipstick. Paul walked behind her and placed a gentle kiss on her Marc Jacob-scented neck while grabbing her thick hips.

She let out a loud moan. "Paul, cut it out."

He continuously flicked his tongue over her neck. "Why are you acting like that in front of my brother?" he asked.

She couldn't speak she just enjoyed the feeling. No one could make her feel the way her husband could. He had *that touch.*

Without saying another word he unzipped her black and gold diamond-encrusted bustier and massaged her big round nipples.

"Step out of those pants," he whispered in her ear.

After doing what she was told, Paul, spread her fat ass cheeks. He got on his knees and sniffed her opening from behind. He loved her scent and couldn't resist sliding his tongue in and out of her ass.

"Oh shit, babe," she moaned, grabbing the top of the dresser.

"Spread that ass, Vix," he said, smacking her cheeks, making her ass jiggle.

He slid his tongue from the back to the front. It felt so good to her that she couldn't control the loud moans that escaped her lips.

"Tell me how that shit feels, Vix."

"Ohhhhh Paul, I'm gonna cum, babe," she cried out.

Paul stood to his feet and unleashed his long, thick shaft and stroked it gently.

Vix grabbed it and squatted low. She opened her mouth as wide as she could and allowed him to fuck her face. Paul loved that his wife could suck him magnificently. When she looked into his eyes and massaged her breasts he sped up his pace. The fact that she didn't gag once turned him on even more.

"Fuck, Vix. No hands, huh?"

She smirked and grabbed the side of his ass and took him in a little deeper. When he felt the back of her throat he knew he was going to give up in a few seconds.

Vix massaged her clit and silently prayed the entire time that she didn't get lock jaw from sucking his long, fat penis like a pro. When he stopped she wanted to shout.

"Bend over," he told her. "And control your moans so the kids won't hear you."

Once she spread her ass again and felt him massage her fat pussy with his magic stick, she threw her ass back so he could go inside of her.

"Ohhhhh," she moaned. "That feels good, honey."

His long, slow strokes took her over the edge.

"What's up with the attitude?" he asked between deep breaths. "Huh?"

"Oh my God, Paul, I'm gonna cum."

He slid out of her and walked over to the bed. When he laid back on it Vix already knew what he was expecting from her. He held his dick in his hands and motioned his finger for her to sit on it. When she straddled him he wanted to scream out like a bitch, but he controlled himself. She squatted and bounced on his dick like an untamed animal, watching her wetness while she rode him took him over the edge.

"Ride your dick, Vix." He leaned up and sucked her breast. The pain that Vix was feeling in her stomach quickly turned into pleasure when she came over his beautiful tool. He grabbed her ass and moved her arm on the side of him while he pounded her until he released all of his seed inside of her.

Vix leaned over and rested on his chest. "Cancel your meeting. I want you to lay here with me."

"It's the first of the month, bae. You know how this shit goes. I gotta make sure my men are straight."

She pouted. When she poked out that bottom lip he couldn't tell her no.

"You're worse than the kids, man." He chuckled.

He reached over to the nightstand and grabbed his phone to send Carstin a text.

Paul: I know you're not into this type of shit, but I need you to be over the meeting today. Just tell them everything I was telling you earlier.

Carstin: My first and last time, nigga. Pussy whipped ass. LOL

Paul: LMAO. Fuck you, man, and I appreciate it.

He looked over to his wife to ask for round two, but she was already sound asleep. He smiled and wrapped his arms around her.

Chapter Four

Vix inserted the house key to her little sister's apartment door lock and let her and Purity in. They were pissed that it was almost one o'clock in the morning and they hadn't arrived at the club yet. They usually didn't get to the club until about one anyway, but because Vanity was taking her precious time, they were going to be even later.

"Y'all hoe's could have knocked," Vanity argued, coming out of her room butt-ass naked.

"Really, Vanity? You're not even dressed?" Vix complained.

"I'm sorry, but I had some last minute dick to come."

Thankfully, her makeup and hair were already done. All she had to do was slip on her dress and shoes and she'd be ready to roll out.

"Which one was it this time?" Vix rolled her eyes.

Vix knew that she'd had her share of men back in her younger days, but her little sister was a straight-up whore. It wasn't because she was insecure; it was simply because she loved men and sex. At first Vix allowed her to do what she felt comfortable doing, but it began to get a bit aggravating because Vanity saw nothing wrong with what she did. Their mother thought that Vanity was a saint, and from Chrystal point of view, Vanity had never had sex.

"Don't hate because you're only getting dick from one man." Vix laughed. "Sorry, P, don't pay me and this fool any mind. What's up with you?"

Purity didn't hear a thing that either of them said because she was too focused tweeting about her upcoming night. She and Vix had gotten dressed at Vix's house and they pregame the entire time. She was feeling good and tipsy.

"Nothing's up. Bring your slow ass on. You know I don't get out much." Purity smiled.

"Exactly," Vix said. Her phone rang and she took it out of her diamond studded clutch. "Hey,

honey. Yes, we're right around the corner. Okay.
Order a bottle of Don Julio please. Okay. Love you."

"What does Paul's ass want?" Vanity asked.

"He's waiting for us, so please hurry up. P and I
will be in the car."

"I'm right behind y'all!" Vanity yelled as Vix
slammed her front door shut.

Every first of the month Paul would rent out the
Bella Noche Night Club just to celebrate being a
young, black, rich nigga. The entire city came out and
had a good time. There were never bad vibes, and
that's what made it more interesting and fun. Paul was
well-respected all over Louisiana so all of his events
always went smooth. He wasn't the type of nigga who
had come up and forgotten where he was from. Paul
had his mansion built right in the hood and he always
had his special events in the hood. Even though
Chrystal couldn't stand her son-n-law she loved that
about him because they were raised up on humbleness.
Vix would've been uncomfortable if Paul had haters
that came for him, but they never had any issues.

"Are you okay?" Purity asked Vix when they got into the car.

"Yes, girl, I'm okay. Vanity just irks my nerves. She's so inconsistent. She knows that my husband likes for me to be on time, but she does this every time."

Vanity climbed into the back seat of Vix's 2016 Porsche Cayenne and popped her gum. "What was said about Vanity?" she asked.

"I said your stupid ass is inconsistent. Every time we go to Paul's celebration week, your ass has me late and that's not a good look because I'm his wife," Vix snapped, clearing the air.

She popped her gum. "Chile, his ass will be alright. You can drive now."

"I bet this'll be the last time I wait for your ass," Vix said, pulling off.

Vanity rubbed her cousin's shoulder from behind. "Purity, we have got to find you a man in here tonight, cousin. These Baton Rouge niggas are the fucking truth."

Purity laughed. "I'm just trying to have a good time tonight, cousin, but whatever happens, happens."

"Oh God, please don't let Vanity turn this girl into a hoe." Vix turned into the club's parking lot, and they all laughed.

"Fuck you, Vix. Don't act like you ain't had a few dicks in your day."

"Lord, I sure have… some good ones too."

They laughed in unison again. The three ladies walked straight through the VIP line with all eyes on them. Men were trying to get at them, and the ladies wanted to be them so bad. The girls in line whispered and adored their beautiful looks. They couldn't believe that three big girls looked that good. BBW's were definitely the shit.

The Louisiana bounce music blasted through the speakers as everyone seemed to go onto the dance floor and twerk like it was their last time. Vanity took a few shots from the bartender's serving tray and threw them back. Purity followed Vix's lead through the club, holding her hand. When Vanity stayed behind and flirted with some dread head, Purity went and grabbed her hand, pulling her toward Paul's VIP section.

Purity laughed and shook her head. "Come on, girl."

"You see that fine-ass nigga?!" Vanity yelled over the loud music, referring to the guy she was flirting with. "I've been wanting to fuck him for a few months now. Tonight may be the night!"

As much as Purity tried to ignore Carstin staring her down, she couldn't. He couldn't ignore her beautiful appearance. The fusion pink and orange fitted dress hugged her thick curves and her fat ass perfectly. When he winked at her, wetness flooded her panties. She quickly took a seat next to Vix and Paul. Vix laughed because she'd been watching the two of them the entire time.

"He's a cutie, isn't he?" Vix asked, whispering in Purity's ear.

"Girl, I have to stay away from him. How come you never told me that Paul had a brother?"

Vix shrugged and sipped on her drink.

"Go sit by him. He won't bite." Vix handed Purity a cup of the expensive liquor.

When she looked over to Carstin who was still staring her down, she threw the entire drink back. She knew she was going to pay for it later, but she didn't care. She needed all the motivation to get next to that man. "Fix me another one," she told Vix. After nursing her second drink, she slowly walked over to Carstin and took a seat next to him.

"I guess I look better sitting over here, huh?" she asked him.

"Hell yeah, you do. You belong over here," he said, making her laugh.

After holding a conversation for a few minutes, Purity immediately felt comfortable around Carstin. She learned that he was twenty-five years old and owned his very own Home Design business. When he told her that he had a bachelor's degree and no kids she could've straddled him down and fucked him right there in front of everybody. It was very rare that you came across a good man that had his shit together so that was definitely a major turn on for Purity.

The song, "Permission" came on, and Purity admired Vix and Paul when they stood up in front of everyone in their section and slow danced. It was the most beautiful thing Purity had ever seen. It was no secret that those two were in love. No matter what they'd been through, they had made it out on top with all smiles, and Purity loved it.

Vanity was on the dance floor slowly throwing her ass back on the guy that she'd been on earlier that night. Just by the looks of her moves, Purity knew that she wasn't lying when she said that they were gonna fuck. On the other hand, she sat there next to Carstin and nursed another drink and laughed at herself. She was one drink away from being sloppy drunk.

Carstin laughed and shook his head because she was weird, but he liked it. He stood up and extended his hand to her. She smiled and shook her head, declining his invitation to dance. When he licked his lips and smiled, she gave in quickly. When Carstin grabbed Purity's left hand and placed it inside of his and grabbed her waist, she threw her arms around his neck and rested her head on his chest.

Lord, he smells so good.

Paul made everyone leave their area. It was just him, Vix, Purity and Carstin. Purity twirled around and pressed her ass against Carstin's dick. Her big, round, plump ass felt so good against him. When she felt his erection, she stepped away from him a bit. She couldn't control the feeling that rushed through her body when he pulled her back into him. She closed her eyes and allowed him do his thing while she continued to sway her hips from left to right. Never in Purity's life had she had allowed a man to get so close to her. She thought about how Aretha could be rolling over in her grave. There she was letting a man she hadn't even known for twenty-four hours touch her in ways only *her* man should've touched her. It actually felt good, though. Purity wasn't sure what had influenced her– the drink or just being tired of being the *good girl*. The best part of it all was it felt like she had known Carstin forever. He was gentle and he had followed her lead the entire time. She enjoyed that.

Purity opened her eyes when she heard a lot of noise coming from the dance floor. When the lights came on in the club, Paul rushed to the dance floor where Vanity and their brother, Tarvis, were. Vix followed her husband, and Carstin ran to catch up with him. Purity slowly walked behind them while holding the pit of her stomach. She felt herself about to throw up any minute, but she wanted to know what was going on with her cousins.

"What's going on, bruh?" Paul asked Tarvis.

"I'm about to take Vanity home. She's embarrassing me in here, man," Tarvis said, grabbing his drunk sister's arm.

She snatched away from him. "Nigga, I'm not embarrassing you. I'm having fun. Let go of my arm."

"You either gon' come with me or I'ma call Mama and let her know what type of hoe you're acting like. Which one?"

She frowned and stormed away from Tarvis.

"Stay away from my little sister, nigga. You already know how we rocking." Tarvis lifted his shirt and showed his gun to the young man that Vanity was entertaining.

Vix and Purity followed Tarvis and Vanity outside and listened to their argument the entire walk to the car.

"You're such a pussy nigga. You're always fucking with me. I don't care about the hoes you fuck with," Vanity snapped.

"You better shut your fat-ass mouth before I bust you in it. Every time your ass goes out, you have to be the main hoe, acting like Mama ain't taught you shit. Those niggas you're fucking with in there are dangerous as fuck, and they don't fuck with me. I'm trying to protect you."

"Y'all, *please* calm down," Vix said, trying control the situation. "It's not that serious, man."

"It *is* that fucking serious, Vix! Shut your ass up!" Tarvis snapped.

"Chill out, bruh," Paul interfered.

Vix wasn't going to argue with Tarvis because she knew how he felt. It wasn't a good look for Vanity to act like a hoe, but Vix could never tell her anything. The fact that she was doing it in public wasn't a good look at all. Vix hated that Vanity was embarrassing their brother and herself.

"Where are you taking her?" Vix asked Tarvis.

"She's going to my house. I'ma let her sleep this shit off so we can talk in the morning because I'm not feeling that shit, and those niggas in there she's fucking around with will get handled, and that's real." He fumed.

"Hit me up in the morning and let me know what's up with them niggas so we can handle that," Paul told him.

Tarvis nodded his head and slapped hands with Paul.

"I love you, bro. Take care of her for me please," Vix said.

"I got to because you damn shol' not." He got into the car and pulled off.

"Oh shit," Purity held her stomach.

"What's wrong, P?" Vix asked.

Purity threw up all over the concrete. When she noticed that Carstin was standing there watching her, she threw up even more. The nervousness and embarrassment didn't mix, but she couldn't help herself.

"I'ma go get her some water." Carstin rushed back into the club.

Vix rubbed her back and comforted her. The night had started out so amazing just to end in a fucked up way. First Tarvis and Vanity had fussed in front of the entire club crowd, and then Purity puked out her entire guts. Paul still felt good. He was just itching to know about those niggas who Tarvis was talking about. If they had a problem with his little brother-n-law, they definitely had a problem with him.

When Carstin gave Purity the water she smiled weakly at him.

"Thanks, handsome. I'm so sorry you had to see me like this."

He took the napkin he held in his hand and wiped her lips.

"Yeah, Carstin, she got a little carried away with the drinks tonight, but she's not like this all the time."

He laughed. "Paul already put me up on the game, sis."

"I'ma head to the house, babe. P isn't feeling good, and I need to get her in bed. When are you coming home?" Vix caressed the side of her husband's face.

He pecked her lips and smacked her fat ass. "Me and bruh right behind y'all. Climb in bed naked for me."

Carstin gently picked Purity up and carried her to Vix's car. She was so drunk she was already asleep in his arms. Vix opened the door for Carstin, and he laid her down on the back seat gently.

Vix smiled at him. "You're so sweet, Carstin." She winked.

"I want her," he returned the smile.

"You might just win her heart if you keep it up, little nigga," Paul said.

They all laughed. Vix got into the car and drove to their house on the south side of town. She really wanted to go to Tarvis' house to get a complete understanding about what was going on with him and the dudes, but she decided to just wait until the next morning. Her head was pounding, and she couldn't wait to get home and snuggle under her sheets.

Chapter Five

Juice walked down the hallway of Tarvis' house in search of Vanity. When he cracked the door open and saw her lying there sound asleep in the guest bedroom he looked back to make sure no one was watching him. The coast was clear so he walked into the room and stood over her. His first mind told him to wake her up with his dick, but the anger inside of him made him cover her mouth with his right hand and grab her throat with the other. Vanity's eyes popped open in complete shock when she saw the angry look on Juice's face. She moved around in the bed and panicked. She wanted to scream, but he covered his lips with his finger signaling her to shut her fucking mouth.

Leaning down, he whispered in her ear, "If you scream I'll hurt you in here."

He stepped back and Vanity quickly sat up in the bed and massaged her neck.

"Are you fucking crazy? Get out of here right now before Tarvis comes," Vanity said through gritted teeth.

Juice leaned back on the dresser and bit his bottom lip.

"He's in the room sleeping. Don't worry about Tarvis."

"You need to leave." Vanity walked into the bathroom. Before she could close the door he stuck his foot in the crack of it. He quickly grabbed her waist and shut the door behind them. She moaned when he reached in front of her and massaged her clit. He loved the feeling of her fat, waxed, pussy. The kisses he planted on her neck and back immediately made her soaking wet.

She turned around and admired his handsome face. She grabbed a few of his dreads and twirled them around on her fingers.

He slapped her hand away from them. "Who the fuck you think you playing with, Vanity?" he asked her in a stern tone.

"I'm not playing with you."

"You a motherfucking lie. You think just because your brother doesn't know that we've been fucking around you can shit on me out here in these streets?"

"I'm not shitting on you, nigga. You knew what it was to begin with. I never wanted to love you. I never wanted to be in love with you. You were fucking me good and next thing I know we were falling in love with each other. That's not what I wanted, and I made that perfectly clear."

"So basically you telling a nigga that you want to be treated like a hoe?"

"Nah. I'm not a hoe." She chuckled, "I'm just having fun."

"You got me fucked up. That lil' nigga you were all over on the dance floor is off limits. He from the other side, and we've had a few shoot outs with that nigga. You belong to me. When I first gave you this dick, what did I say?"

"That this was yours and yours only."

"Okay. If I even *think* you fucking another nigga. I'ma fuck you up. Do you hear me?"

"I'm not fucking scared of you, Juice." She grinned, wickedly. "Your threats don't scare me," she whispered and winked.

"That ain't a threat. It's a promise. Ask your brother who's the first one to pull a trigger out the click." He winked back.

When he dug into his pockets Vanity's heartbeat sped up. She felt relieved when he didn't pull out the gun, but she could've fallen back into the bathtub when she saw the pregnancy test in his hand. The look on Vanity's face was priceless, and Juice loved it.

He tossed it to her. "Pee."

Her eyes watered and she yelled, "Nigga, you got me fucked up!"

"What you crying for?"

"Because I'm not pregnant. Why do I have to pee on a stick?"

"If you're not pregnant then it shouldn't be a problem to pee. Who do you think you're talking to? Pee on the motherfucking stick."

She wiped the tears from her eyes.

"Lord, Jesus, *please*," she prayed before she squatted over the stool.

Vanity already knew what the test was going to say. She hadn't seen her period in two months. She was afraid to take the pregnancy test that Vix offered her a while back so she just made herself believe that she wasn't.

After peeing on the stick and waiting for a few minutes her heart almost sunk when the pregnancy test read positive. She burst into tears, "No, this isn't right!" She sniffled.

"Open your legs to another nigga while you're pregnant with my seed and watch what happens," he threatened.

"You don't even know if the baby is yours."

"You and I know that baby is mine. I'll see you tomorrow." He kissed her forehead and walked out of the bathroom.

When Vanity heard the front door shut she fell onto the floor and cried like a little baby. "I can't have this baby." She climbed back into the bed and cried herself back to sleep.

Purity woke up to the sound of her alarm and quickly panicked when she noticed that she wasn't home in her bed.

"Oh, shit." She sat up in the bed. "Where the hell am I?" she questioned. Her head pounded from a hangover. She lay back in the bed and tried to remember the night before. She knew that she'd gone out with Vanity and Vix and had a lot of drinks at the club, but she couldn't remember what happened at the end of the night.

When the door opened and she heard footsteps, she almost fell out the bed when she saw Carstin's fine, muscular, beautiful ass walk through the door.

"What the hell?" She finally looked around and remembered that she was at Vix's house. "What are you doing in here?" she asked, covering her naked body with the sheets.

"Vix told me to come and wake you up for breakfast. Are you a'ight?" He sat at the foot of the bed.

"No. What time is it and why are you in here? I don't know you like that."

"It's eleven-thirteen. You good?" He ignored her extra comments.

"I'm fine. Can you get out so I can freshen up?"

He chuckled and stood up. "Yeah, little mama. I'll be back to check on you, though. You need anything?"

"Some water and a BC, please," She smiled.

Purity rushed into the bathroom and turned on the shower. She looked in the mirror and couldn't believe that she had allowed herself to get so carried away at the club. Besides the headache that was kicking her ass, she actually felt good for a change. Usually, on Saturday mornings she would be at her desk with a cup of hot coffee doing work, but not today.

She stepped into the shower, closed the shower door, and allowed the steaming hot water to run down her back and over her entire body. The feeling was completely unexplainable. She needed that and she immediately felt awakened.

"Vix!" she called out when the bathroom door opened. Without thinking, she opened the shower door and her mouth fell wide open when she saw Carstin.

"Oh my God! Get out of here, nigga!" She tried to cover her big body with her arms and hands.

Carstin bit down on his bottom lips and looked her up and down. "Damn, you fine as fuck."

Her mouth hung wide open again. "Is this shit real? Are you really standing in here watching me shower like you know me?"

"I just came to bring you the BC and water. You're acting like a nigga never saw you naked before. Damn." He frowned.

"A man has never seen me naked before. *Never.* And even if a man did see me naked I don't know your ass from a can of paint. What kind of girl do you think I am?"

"A girl who needs some good dick in your life. You uptight as fuck."

He walked out of the bathroom, leaving her in complete shock. She continued to wash her body and thought about what he'd said. She was surprised that he didn't feel disgusted by her little rolls and dimples. She knew that she was a big girl and most men tried their best to do and say anything to get in the bed with girls like her so she wasn't going for it. She planned to pretend that what had just happened never happened.

***

Carstin sat at the island and watched Paul and Vix interact with each other. They loved on each other like they had just met, and Carstin loved that shit.

"What happened when you went upstairs?" Paul asked him.

"I walked in the bathroom while she was showering. She almost pissed on herself."

"You did *what*?!" Vix yelled.

Paul could have died from laughter.

"Uh-uh, Paul! Don't laugh at him. Let me go check on my cousin. She's probably up there scared out her mind."

"She ain't scared. Her eyes were on the print of my dick the entire time."

Vix giggled. "Oh my God."

When Vix walked toward the stairs Vanity came rushing in like a mad woman. She was dressed in grey sweat pants, a purple LSU t-shirt, and her long thick hair was sticking straight up.

"Vanity?" she rushed to her sister, "What's wrong with you? What happened?"

Wiping her tears, Vanity said, "I really need to talk to you in private."

"Take those biscuits out the oven, babe," Vix demanded. "Let me go holler at my sister."

The two of them walked up the stairs as Purity was coming down. When she saw Vanity crying, she turned around and followed them into the master bedroom.

In a pleading tone, Vix begged, "Tell me what's going on, sis."

Vanity burst out into tears. "Why me, Lord?" She cried harder.

"Vanity, you're scaring me. What's wrong? You have AIDS or something?"

"Vix!" Purity pushed her arm.

"I'm pregnant, and it's Juice's baby."

"You're *what*?! And it's *whose* baby?" Purity asked, making sure she'd heard it right.

Vix shook her head. "No, Vanity, *no*! You've been sleeping with Juice? Are you fucking serious?"

"Please don't be mad with me, Vix. We were just fucking and then our feelings grew attached. I told him we were doing it too much, man. I told him."

"Don't you dare blame that man, Vanity! You knew better than to have sex with Tarvis best friend," Purity snapped.

"P, shut up. I don't need your fucking holy speeches," Vanity snapped and turned toward her sister.

"No, she's right, Van. You know that Juice and Tarvis have been boys since they were kids. Out of all the niggas you could've fucked, you fucked his right-hand man and you're pregnant. Tarvis is going to kill him."

"You took a test?" Purity asked.

"Girl, he came to Tarvis' house last night when I was asleep. This nigga is crazy as fuck. He told me that I was playing him and I had him fucked up if I thought I was going to be fucking around on him. He's obviously been paying attention to my body because he passed me a pregnancy test."

"Damn! If he knew you didn't have your period, that means y'all had to be fucking up a storm," Purity pointed out.

"Man, we fuck every other day," Vanity admitted.

"What are you going to do?" Vix asked her.

"I want to get an abortion, but he'll kill me. He acted like he was happy about me being pregnant or some shit. I can't have no fucking baby, man. This is going to be so much drama."

"So you was just letting the nigga nut in you?" Vix questioned.

The silence was confirmation that she had allowed it.

"Wow, Vanity. I don't know what to tell you. Get prepared for motherhood."

"This nigga don't even want this baby. He just wanna lock me down." She wiped her tears. "It wasn't supposed to be like this. I'm in love with this nigga and I don't want to be. I try sleeping with different men to take the feelings away, but it just doesn't work. Now on top of this I'm pregnant. This is all bad."

"Wow. I can't believe that you've been keeping a secret like this from me."

Vix felt betrayed. She told her sister all of her secrets and she expected her to do the same. She felt bad that there wasn't a thing she could do to fix the situation for Vanity, but she'd done it to herself. She knew that someone was going to get hurt because Tarvis didn't play about his baby sister and the fact that they were being sneaky behind his back didn't make it better.

"You don't think I can get an abortion and just make him think I lost the baby?"

"No, you're not getting an abortion, so stop saying that. That shit will haunt you. I know this."

Vanity burst into tears again. Purity and Vix actually felt bad for her. She looked so pitiful. Vix always tried to warn her about moving so fast and that was a reason why right there.

"My brother is going to be so disappointed in me," Vanity admitted.

"Girl, disappointed is an understatement. He's going to put his hands on you."

The three of them laid back in bed. Purity and Vix were in complete shock when she told them everything about her and Juice. No one would've ever thought that Juice would be in love with Vanity.

Chapter Six

Juice pulled into his mother's driveway and put his car in park when he saw his sister and her boyfriend arguing in front of the house. The argument was so big they didn't even realize that he had pulled up.

"You put me on child support just to receive food stamps and checks? You broke bitch!" JT yelled, scaring Sheika.

"No, nigga, I put your whack ass on child support because you don't do shit for my son. You think just because I work hard that you don't have to do shit? You got me fucked me," she snapped.

"Fuck you and that little nigga," JT said just before he walked off.

Juice jumped out of his car and walked toward JT. When JT noticed the gun that Juice had pulled out he pissed on himself.

Juice took the butt of his gun and hit JT in the nose as hard as he could. He fell on the ground and tried to cover his face, but Juice was already on his ass fucking him up.

"Fuck who, nigga?" he asked between hits. "You disrespect my sister, fuck nigga?" He dropped the gun and began to beat him with his fist.

Sheika pulled on his shirt."Juice, stop it! You're going to kill him. Mama!" Sheika yelled for help.

"What the hell? Juice! Get off that boy right now!" Their mother ran to him and pushed him off of JT. "What the hell is going on out here, Sheika?" Sonya asked.

"JT you need to go." Sheika tried to give him a hand, and Juice pushed her.

"I wish you fucking would help that nigga after the way he just disrespected you."

She wiped her tears. "But, Juice, look at how you did him. You could've killed him."

"I should've." Juice walked toward the house.

"I get so fucking sick of this shit, Sheika! He needs to get his ass away from here and you can leave too. I don't have time for this. Every time I turn around it's some shit!" Sonya argued.

As long as Sonya could remember, Juice was always getting into trouble for his sister who didn't give a damn about anyone but herself. Juice would beat JT's ass for Sheika, and she would be right back with him, but Juice didn't care. If his sister wanted to be with that nigga that was fine, but disrespecting her in front of him was not cool.

Juice flopped down on his mama's sofa and massaged his swollen knuckles. He was glad that he thought before he pulled that trigger like he wanted to.

Grabbing her cigarettes off the counter top, Sonya argued, "Your sister is going to send you straight to prison! You know that?"

"As long as I'm living a nigga will never in life disrespect mine. I don't care about going to prison when it comes to Sheika. You know this."

Sonya shook her head. Arguing with her hot-head son wouldn't change a thing, so she left it alone. She lit her cigarette and sat next to her one and only son.

"I know you love her, Juice, but Sheika is going to have to learn that man doesn't care about her or my grandson. She only put him on them papers because he hadn't been paying her ass any attention. I didn't raise Sheika to be so weak, man."

"Sheika ain't weak, Ma. She's just in love. She'll get it, though."

"Keep on thinking that. What brought you by?"

Juice sighed and put his face in his hands. He wasn't sure if he should bring Vanity's pregnancy up after what had just happened, but he needed to get the situation off his chest. He hadn't talked to anyone about it, and he knew that his secret was safe with his mama.

"I'm in a tough situation right now, Ma."

She sat up. "What's the matter, son?"

"Don't judge a nigga and please don't flip out. Vanity and I have been creeping around, and she's pregnant."

"Say fucking what!" She jumped up.

"Why are you so loud?"

"Vanity and you are having an affair and she's pregnant? What? I thought Chrystal said Vanity was still a virgin?"

Juice frowned. "A *virgin*?"

"Yeah. At least that's the impression she's been giving her mama."

"Vanity ain't no damn virgin, Ma. And I wasn't the first nigga to bust that open, but that ain't your business. I'm just messed up right now. Tarvis doesn't know."

Sonya sighed and shook her head. "Lord, have mercy, Jesus! My children are going to send me straight to my grave." She smoked her cigarette down and sparked another one. "When did all this shit happen? Out of all the skanks you could be messing with around here, why did you go after Vanity? I really want to slap your ass because y'all was raised up together almost like fucking cousins."

"I always liked Vanity's ratchet ass, man. I don't know. I just love her ass. I love her because she's herself, and she's a beast in bed."

"Oh, Lord!" she said, covering her ears. "I don't want to even picture that."

Juice laughed. "You asked."

"You really in love with her?" Sonya asked, surprised that her son had finally admitted to loving a woman.

"I'm in love with this girl, but I think we moved too fast. I didn't mean to knock her up. Now I'ma have to deal with her brother and her stupid ass. I would hate to lose my best friend behind this shit."

"You should've never crept with her then."

"How do you think Chrystal is gonna feel about this?"

"I have no idea. I know that she loves you like you're her own child and she thinks the sun sets on

Vanity, but I don't know. I'm disappointed in y'all, though."

"I know. How do you think I should handle Tarvis?"

"Talk with Vanity first and see how she feels about it and how she wants to handle it."

"Damn, man." He shook his head. "This is crazy."

"I can't believe it." Sonya stared off and finished her cigarette.

"Vanity's always been your favorite, though. What's the big deal?"

"She has always been my favorite, but damn. That's too close to home, and I know it's about to be some shit between you and Tarvis and I don't have time for it."

"That nigga will be alright. I'ma handle it right whenever I do decide to handle it."

"Keep on thinking you can solve everything."

Ignoring his mother and placing a big kiss on her cheek, he said, "I'll be over here tomorrow. Keep an eye out on Sheika please."

"I hear you. Call me and keep me posted with everything." She walked him outside.

Juice drove to Ruth's Chris Steak House to get Vanity's favorite dishes. Over the few months he had spent with her, he had learned that it was her favorite place to eat. While driving, his phone started ringing off the hook. Whoever was calling would have to wait. Juice just couldn't make himself believe that he was in love with Vanity and she was going to have his baby. He knew that she was living and doing her things in the streets and he vowed to never fall for her when they started creeping around. But she made it so hard. He enjoyed being around her because she wasn't aggravating like the other women he dealt with. She was herself around him or away from him. He liked the fact that she could control him in the bedroom. She had the best pussy ever and she always catered to him after their sex sections. He would've felt like a pussy nigga if the feelings weren't mutual, but he knew that she was in love with him.

He went into the restaurant and ordered the food. He ordered Vanity pork chops, mash potatoes, creamy spinach, and cheesecake. He ordered the stuffed chicken breast and a baked potato for himself. Juice thought about calling Vanity before he went over to her house, but he wanted to pop up to see if she was doing something she had no business doing.

As much as Juice hated that Vanity lived in Indigo Park, he had no choice but to get used to it. He had way too many female friends in that apartment complex and he wouldn't be surprised if any drama were to pop off.

Instead of having respect and knocking, he placed the key that he had made into the door lock. When he walked in and entered the dining room, Vanity could've pissed on herself. And if looks could kill, Vanity would've been dead.

"How the fuck did you get in here, Juice?"

"I got a fucking key made. Who the fuck is this nigga?" He pointed to the guy sitting down at the table.

"Don't you dare talk to Jacob like that, nigga. This is my fucking study partner."

"Oh…okay… Well, she'll holler at you, Jacob from State Farm. Study time is over."

As scared as Jacob was he couldn't help but laugh. "We were wrapping it up anyway. Thanks for the study, Van." He hurried out of the house.

Juice placed the bags on the table and walked over to Vanity. "You missed me?" He kissed her neck.

"No, Juice. How'd you get that key?"

"Don't worry about how I got my key. I had to make some shit shake since you wouldn't give me one."

"That's because you don't need one. I'm not your woman, Juice."

"But you my baby mama."

Hearing him say that made tears immediately well up in her eyes. "Can you just stop saying that shit? Stop it!"

"What the fuck you mean, Vanity? It's the truth. You're pregnant with my baby and that's all it is to it."

She sat down at the table and put her head on it. She cried and Juice hated that shit.

"I'm not ready for this, Juice. Tarvis is going to hate me and he's going to kill you. I think you did this to me on purpose."

"Man, I ain't do shit on purpose and don't trip on Tarvis. I got him."

"You don't know my brother." She shook her head.

"I know your brother better than *you* do."

Vanity's phone vibrated and Juice picked it up.

"Give me my phone!" She reached.

"Get back." He clicked on the message.

Jacob: Damn, you giving him some of my pussy too?

When Juice frowned at Vanity she knew that he had seen something he shouldn't have.

Vanity: Nah, nigga. This is MY pussy. You don't have to worry about the little study sessions no more.

He stuffed the phone inside his pocket. "How many niggas you fucking out here, Vanity?"

"That's none of your business. Who was that?"

"That was Jake from State Farm. If I see that pussy nigga around this house again, I'ma kill him and you. You hear me?"

She rolled her eyes, and sarcastically."Yes, Daddy."

"That a girl."

Vanity went into the bags and smiled when she saw all of her favorite meal.

"What did I do to deserve this?"

"I should take my shit back and eat it in your face."

She smiled at him. "Don't be like that. Pass me the salt."

That was what he loved the most. No matter what the situation was, they always ended up in good spirits.

Chapter Seven

The sound of Vix's heels on the floor alerted Hazel that she had come into the house. He had to be in the shower when she opened the door because he didn't hear the alarm system go off.

"Hazel!" Vix called his name.

She looked around his big, beautiful home and hadn't much changed. He was still a simple person.

"I'm upstairs! Come here real quick!"

Vix knew that being at Hazel's house was the worst thing that she could do while her husband was out of town, but she couldn't resist being in his presence just for a few minutes. When Vix found out that Paul was having an affair while he was in prison, she fell for Hazel so easily. It was almost liked she never loved Paul. The way Hazel made her feel and the way he treated her was right on time. She couldn't decide which man as the better lover because Paul and

Hazel were beasts in bed. Hazel knew for a fact that Vix would leave Paul and be with him in the beginning of their secret relationship, but he had it all wrong. The power that Paul had over Vix was too much and Hazel knew that when she aborted their child. Even though the procedure broke his heart, he still loved the shit out of her. They hadn't had any dealings with each other since Paul was released from prison, but Vix was anxious to know why he had gone out of his way to contact Vanity just to get her to come over so she had to see what was up.

When she walked into his bedroom and saw him lying on the bed with only boxers on, her flood gates opened. His print showed so perfectly, and it brought back memories. She stood in the door way with her legs crossed and hands clutching her purse.

He patted the space next to him. "Come sit right here."

Vix did as she was told and stared at Hazel. The love was definitely there in the room, but all she could think about was her husband.

"Why'd you call me here, Hazel? What's up?"

"I wanted to see you, and you came. So that means you wanted to see me too. Am I wrong?"

She shook her head.

He sat up in the bed and checked her out. "As always, you look beautiful."

She rocked her two-piece floral skirt and crop top so graciously. Even though she was more on the big girl side, she always kept herself at a great size. She wasn't scared to wear what she wanted to wear, and she wasn't scared to show off her skin. Hazel loved that, and he had yet to find another woman who was comfortable in their own skin like Vix.

"Thank you. You don't look too bad." She smirked.

"It's been a long time."

"It has been. And we both know that I'm breaking all the codes by being here."

Scooting next to her, he asked, "Can I be honest with you?"

"Please."

"Fuck your husband. Whatever you and I do is between us, and it always will be unless you tell him like you did the last time. I ain't ever been scared to fight for you, but I know you love that nigga. I just want you here with me today, though. Just this one time. Let me fuck you and cater to you just one more time and that'll be it for—"

Cutting him off with a kiss, she allowed him to reach under her skirt and gently slide her panties down. He slowly took her shoes off and massaged her toes. Vix was at a loss for words as she watched him take over like she belonged to him. She couldn't say anything because her throbbing cat didn't want her to. At that point she wanted to be fucked and think about all the consequences later. She allowed him to undress her and lay back on the bed.

He admired her beautiful, tattooed body. He kissed her from her toes to her legs, and slowly licked on her thighs.

"Mmm," she moaned.

He spread her legs and kissed on her inner thighs, causing her to squirm. He slipped his tongue into her opening, causing her to scream out in pleasure.

"Oh, shit."

When she looked down at him and saw him eating her and staring into her eyes she covered her face. Yes, she was shame. Paul hadn't done anything to be cheated on, but there she was getting her pussy catered to by another man that she once loved.

Is this shit really happening? She thought.

The way he sucked on her clit sent chills down her spine. She could feel her juices sliding to the crack of her ass. He continuously sucked on her clit until she couldn't take it anymore. She came so hard and the proof was right there in his long, thick beard.

He took his boxers off and his dick was standing straight in the air. The first way he took her was in between her thighs. He loved that she wasn't stiff. After throwing both of her thick thighs over his shoulders he gently pushed himself inside of her tight, wet opening.

"Shittttt," she dragged.

The slow thrusting took her over the edge.

"Speed up just a little bit," she whispered in his ear. "Just a little bit."

He leaned up and gave her all of him. The white cum covering his manhood turned him on even more. She scratched his back with her long nails, but that didn't matter at the moment. Her pussy was too good to focus on that.

"You missed this, didn't you?" he sucked on her bottom lip.

"Yesssssss!" she screamed while cumming again.

"I missed this shit too."

After he pulled out and lay back on the bed, Vix turned backwards and road him. Her fat ass made his entire dick disappear.

"Shit, Vix."

He licked his thumb and slowly placed it into her asshole.

"Awwww, shit, Hazel. I'm gonna cum again."

He slapped her ass. "Come on."

When she slowed down, Hazel leaned forward and pushed her.

"Arch your back," he demanded.

She arched her back and spread her ass wide. He slowly ate her from the back.

"Hazel, what are you doing to me?" she moaned.

He roughly shoved himself inside of her, making her pussy make loud noises.

"Winning your heart again," he said right before he let off the biggest load on her ass.

Vix laid there with her mouth wide open. Everything had happened so fast, and her body felt so good. The sex was so amazing she actually felt her pussy throb just from thinking about it. The amazing sex didn't make her stop thinking about Paul, though.

She immediately felt guilty and the tears that rolled down her face were confirmation.

When Hazel heard the sniffling, he asked, "What's wrong, Vix?"

"My husband," she responded, wiping her tears.

Hearing her say that after their bomb-ass sex definitely made him feel some type of way, but he knew the deal from the beginning. He was going to do anything to make her understand that she belonged with him.

"What he don't know won't hurt him."

"But—"

"Sshh," he said, quickly cutting her off. "Get up and let me wash you off."

With tears still falling from her eyes, Vix tried to smile and make Hazel think she was okay. She followed him into the shower and allowed him to take care of her.

"Would you believe me if I said that you still own my heart?" He washed her back off.

"After the way you just fucked me, I think I would." They laughed. "But, Hazel, really, I can't do this with you. Paul's a good man. I love him."

"And you love me too, don't you?"

She turned and looked at him."What if I told you no?"

"Then you'd be lying."

"And you know this because?"

"Your pussy said so, and I can look and see that little sparkle in your eye. I'm not trying to rush you or make you do anything you don't want to do, but let's see how it all goes. Okay?"

She nodded her head and began to wash him off.

Vix waited until Hazel was asleep before she got up and put on her clothes. She quickly got into her car and rushed over to Vanity's house at two o'clock in the morning. She was glad that the kids were with her mother and that Paul had only called to check on her twice. When she pulled up to Vanity's apartment, she ran up the stairs and let herself in. She was grateful that Vanity was asleep and not in bed having sex with God knows who. She flicked on the lights and crawled into bed with her.

"Vanity," she gently shook her.

"What? What time is it?" she asked her, trying to avoid opening her eyes.

"I really need to talk to you. I think I fucked up."

She walked out of the room and into the living room. She checked her phone and wanted to call her husband so bad and just apologize, but she knew better.

"This better be some serious shit, man. I was sleeping so good."

"I'm surprised you don't have any company over here. You must be scared of Juice." She giggled.

"Shut the hell up. I'm not scared of no damn body. What's up? What's wrong?"

"I fucked Hazel."

Vanity eyes widened and her mouth fell open. "You did *what*?"

"I fucked him and that's not it."

"Man, I don't think I wanna hear nothing else."

"I think I'm still in love with him. Have you ever been away from someone that you've loved and thought the feelings were gone and you come back around them and the love and feelings are still there? That's my situation."

"Damn, Vix. I thought you were in love with your husband."

"Bitch, I am!" Vix snapped. She was offended.

"Well, of course you are. That's why I didn't think you would cheat on him. Y'all have been doing good. How was the sex with Hazel?"

"Girl, he made me cum about ten times back to back. I couldn't feel my toes. I couldn't control it."

Vanity laughed. "Oh my God. Ten times? Girl, I don't think I've ever had sex that bomb. Are you serious?" She laughed harder. Vanity immediately regretted joking with her sister when she saw tears falling from eyes. "Wait. You're crying?"

"This isn't funny, Vanity. Be serious for a minute. What'd I do?"

"I'm sorry for laughing, but I don't know what to tell you, sis. What do you want to do?"

"I really want to see him more, but I know that's not what I should do. I love my husband to pieces, but sometimes I feel so insecure after knowing he stepped out on me and got that bitch, Melissa, pregnant. A part of me feels like I owe Hazel for breaking his heart. I just couldn't have that baby, though."

"Well, I'ma just say this, Vix. You chose to stay with Paul after his affair he so you can't use that as an excuse to do your dirt, especially if he's doing everything he needs to do in your marriage now. I would tell you to do whatever your heart tells you to do, but that's obviously fucking with Hazel on the side and you can't do that. Hell, if you weren't married it wouldn't be so bad, but you're playing with fire. Paul will kill you."

"Damn, you're right, man."

"But you already know I always loved Hazel more than your husband."

Vix threw the pillow at her, changing the subject. "Shut, up and make us some chicken tacos."

Vix felt at peace being around her sister, and she was so grateful for their bond. No matter what they went through, they could always count on each other.

She followed Vanity into the kitchen. "Have you and Juice decided how y'all are going to handle this whole thing?"

"We're gonna tell Mama first and then Tarvis."

"I'ma be locked in my room when that shit goes down. Mama's gon' be heartbroken. She thinks you're a saint."

"I know, but shouldn't they want someone like Juice to be with me instead of one of these knuckleheads?"

"Girl, me and you both know that Juice ain't shit and ain't no telling what Tarvis knows that we don't."

"You're right. But I ain't shit either, though, so who am I to judge?"

Vix burst out in laughter.

"What? Shit, I'm serious."

"I know, but did your crazy ass have to say it like that?"

"Yeah, but let's just focus on the positive right now."

They got caught up in different subjects to take their minds off of the bullshit while they prepared the food.

***

Paul looked at his phone and shoved it back inside his pocket. He was trying his best to give Melissa all of his attention while they were away on vacation, but of course that wasn't possible because his workers couldn't seem to get shit done without him.

The wind was blowing and the sound of the waves was relaxing, but he couldn't enjoy the trip even if he wanted to.

"Who's calling, babe? Wifey?" Melissa asked, sarcastically.

"Nah, that ain't her. Just those dumb-ass niggas that I call my workers."

"Can we just focus on this amazing view? This was supposed to be our time together. Remember?"

"How can I forget when your fine ass is reminding me every ten seconds?" He picked her up, tickling her all over her body. "You're a beautiful-ass girl. You know that, right?"

"Yes." She pecked his lips. "Thanks for always reminding me of that every ten seconds." She smiled.

"I got to."

Melissa was a beautiful Jamaican who stood at 5'3".She ran away from him and got into the water. That gave him enough time to smoke a blunt and check in with Vix."Hello?" she answered the phone.

"I'm missing you, thickums."

She giggled. "I'm missing you too, babe."

"You alright? You need anything?"

"I'm good, honey. Just patiently waiting for you to come back home."

"I love you," he told her.

"I love you too."

"I'ma call you after I leave this meeting," he lied.

"Okay. Be careful."

Paul hung up the phone and shook his head. He hated the fact that he had to lie to his wife, but he had to do anything in his power to keep Melissa happy. Vix was under the impression that Paul went to Jamaica to meet with his plug, but that lie was to throw her off. Melissa's daddy was Paul's plug and whenever she was happy with him Paul got all of his product for the low. Paul was far from broke, but being that he didn't have to spend thousands a month on products, made shit so much easier. He wasn't in love with Melissa, but she came in handy. Sometimes it broke his heart that he was cheating on his wife with the bitch that had brought so much pain to their marriage to begin with, but sometimes you had to do what you had to do.

One thing he always did was wrap his dick up whenever he was fucked her. And he never made love to her the way he made love to Vix.

"Come get in the water with me!" Melissa yelled.

Paul took off his shirt and shorts and slowly walked into the water. Melissa jumped into his arms and wrapped her legs around his waist and kissed him all over his face.

She was so in love with Paul that words couldn't even explain it, but of course she couldn't see that he didn't care for her ass much. He wished that she was an obedient side bitch and just accepted dick every now and then, but she knew just what to do. If he even thought about leaving her alone, she would tell his wife everything without a second thought.

"I love you, Paul."

He smiled. "I know."

After their long swim and bonding in the water, they went back to the hotel room to freshen up for dinner. The staff at the Grand Palladium Resort had treated them so well. Melissa didn't want their trip to come to an end. The view was perfect. Paul didn't give a fuck about it, but it meant everything to her. Paul thought that having dinner on the beach was reserved for couples who really loved each other, but of course he was doing whatever Melissa wanted to do. Hell, if she wanted dinner in the water, he would make it happen so he could have everything he needed from her father by the end of the month.

He knew that all of the creeping he was doing would pay off in the end. He just had to find a way to cut Melissa off without all of the drama and chaos in the end.

Chapter Eight

Carstin walked into the courtroom where Purity had been assigned to for the day. If she was a basic broad that he was just trying to fuck, he would've never gone out of his way to bring flowers and chocolates to her job. The courtroom was jammed pack, but that didn't stop everyone from staring a hole through him when he walked over to the bench to sit down. When Purity locked eyes with him, all she could do was blush. For the first time, ever, she was distracted. Regaining her composure, she quickly snapped back to work. It was hard to believe that there had been over one hundred people to get locked up the night before. Purity typed so much that day her wrists were killing her and she couldn't wait until she saw five o'clock in the corner of her computer screen.

Even though Purity was nervous that Carstin was sitting right there staring her down, she had to focus. She wasn't going to allow him to think that he had that much juice, so she tuned him out. Paul was patiently sitting watching her every move. She was fast, and he liked that. While all the women that were sitting around him were staring and whispering about how fine he was, he still wasn't focused on any of them. He paid close attention to who he had come there for.

Two hours later, Purity finally closed her computer and prepared to leave the stand. The courtroom was empty, leaving only the workers, and Carstin there.

"You should really take a vacation sometimes, Purity. You work so hard," Judge Messer suggested.

"I don't have enough of a life to take off from work for a vacation, sir."

"Come into work thirty minutes early in the morning, will you? I'll have my wife to set something up for you. She's a travel agent."

"You don't even have to do that."

She said goodbye to everyone and walked toward Carstin who was now standing and smiling.

"Hey, Carstin."

"Hey, Purity."

"You know if I wasn't mistaking, I would say that you're harassing me."

He chuckled. "If that's what you call trying to get a little of your time, then I'm all for it."

"Seriously, what brought you up here?"

He waved the flowers and the big chocolate candy box in her face.

"Are you not used to shit like this?"

"No," she admitted.

"I can tell. I brought you these because I felt you deserved them. To get straight to the point, a nigga wanna get to know you better and spend some time with you. It seems like you're scared for some odd reason, but don't be. You can loosen up around me."

She smiled. "If you hadn't walked in on me naked, I would call you a gentleman."

The shared a laugh.

"I do apologize for doing that, but I wanted to see your reaction."

"You better be glad I didn't have my gun on me. I probably would've shot you."

They walked outside to Purity's car and held casual conversation.

"I really have to go. I'm supposed to meet Paul and Vix at their house so that they can take me house hunting."

"He sent me to do that." He smirked.

"I should've known they were up to something." She laughed. "Well, okay. How about I hop in with you? I'm too tired to drive."

He took her hand and kissed it. "That was the plan."

Purity was trying hard to not fall for him, but he didn't make the task easy. He was everything a woman could ask for as far as she knew. He was sexy, a gentleman, he wasn't involved with any illegal activities, and he was funny. For a long time Purity had made herself believe that God didn't want her with anyone at the moment, but that quickly changed when Carstin continuously came around. Even though they hadn't spent any time alone, he was like a breath of fresh air. Whenever he was at Vix's house, she would make her way over there just to see his face. She couldn't even count how many times that she masturbated while wishing that it was Carstin touching her instead.

He opened the door for her, and she got in and kicked off her shoes.

"Make yourself at home then." He laughed, getting into the driver's seat.

"I might as well. That's what you want me to do, right?"

"Exactly."

Instead of blasting the music how he normally would, he decided that a conversation would be better.

"You're good at what you do," he told her.

"Huh?"

"Your job. You move fast as hell. I watched you for two whole hours and you didn't slack one time. I like that."

"Thank you. I love being a court reporter. It's interesting as hell, and I learn a lot. Those cases teach me so much."

He nodded in agreement.

"So tell me when was the last time a man took you out."

"To be honest with you, Carstin, I've never been on a date. *Never*. I never even had a boyfriend."

"Say what?"

"Nope. It's the truth. That's a turn off, huh?"

"Hell nah that's not a turn off. As beautiful as you are, I'm surprised to hear some shit like that. You lying to a nigga?"

"No need to lie to you. I've never had a boyfriend and I don't have any guy friends. I suffered from low self-esteem for a very long time. I'm trying to step out of the box and do a few things to loosen up, but I'm what they call a *good girl*."

"So I take it that you never had sex?"

She shook her head. "Never."

"Wow," he said, gripping the wheel and focusing on the road.

It didn't take long for a million things to rush through his head. He'd never taken the time to think about if that was something he could handle. Well, in his mind he was ready for a good woman, but he suddenly thought what could happen if he got with Purity and fucked it up. He never wanted to be the nigga to hurt a good girl's feelings, and in the past that was all he ever did. But he was ready.

For the rest of the evening they rode around the entire city of Baton Rouge looking at homes. It was one house that Purity liked and it wasn't too far from her grandmother's house. But it looked so broken down and raggedy on the inside. Carstin parked in the front of it and took a look around.

"This house is big as fuck. You don't like it?" he asked her.

The twisting of her lips and rising of her eyebrows told him her answer.

"It's nice, but look how it looks from the outside. You can look through the windows and tell it's worn down."

"Come on. Let's go walk up close and see."

They walked hand and hand up close to the house. She was right. When they peaked into the window, the house looked worn down, but it was nothing a little work couldn't do.

"If this is what you want, it can be hooked up. I think it's nice."

"By the time I finish fixing this house up I'll be dead broke. I think we should look for something that's not so bad."

"Nah, I'ma make some shit shake. If this is what you like, it can be fixed up."

"Carstin, I'm not trying to break your pockets." She giggled.

"I own a design business, P. You won't break my pockets. And since you're my new girl and all, it's the least I can do." He smiled.

"*Your girl*, huh?" She blushed.

He kissed her cheek and threw his arm around her shoulder. "You heard me right, baby."

"Let's go eat, man. Fucking with you a nigga gone die from starvation."

***

As their night slowly cam to an end, Purity didn't want to leave Carstin's side. He made her laugh until her stomach was in knots, and she smiled until her cheeks hurt the entire time they were at dinner. Cheesecake Bristo was mad packed, but that didn't stop them from enjoying themselves. Purity couldn't believe that she had loosened up around Carstin so fast. He was everything, and if she could stay around him forever, she would. He made her so comfortable that she confided in him about her broken relationship with Tawny.

"I really enjoyed myself tonight, Carstin." She blew a kiss.

"Alright now. Blowing a kiss like that will get you in trouble."

She giggled. "Oh, God. Whatever." She threw her napkin at him.

"Let me get you home. I know you have to work tomorrow."

She nodded in agreement.

Carstin took her hand and allowed her to walk in front of him. The wait line for seating was ridiculous, and Purity was glad they'd gotten in when they did.

"Erika?" Carstin looked to make sure his eyes weren't playing tricks on him. It was her, her sister, and her mother. When Purity noticed that Carstin knew the pregnant woman that was standing by the entrance she stopped and looked at the two of them exchange small conversation.

She smiled weakly. "Um, Carstin. Hey."

"What you doing here?" he asked her.

"She's here for school. Now if you don't mind we were just getting ready to have dinner."

Carstin threw his hands up in surrender. Erika's mother could never stand Carstin and he never gave a fuck. Erika and Carstin were in a relationship for a few months before he left Jackson. He was feeling Erika but he couldn't deal with the mind control that her parents had over her. It was almost like he was dating a child so he fell back from her. Of course her mother thought he was a dog-ass street nigga because he took her virginity and didn't put a ring on her finger. He would be lying if he said that he wasn't caught off guard. And the fact that she was pregnant fucked him up a little bit.

Carstin waved and grabbed Purity's hand. "I'll see you around I guess, Erika."

"Who was that?" Purity asked.

"My ex."

"I thought you didn't have people here? You're lying to me already?"

"Nah, you heard her say she came here for school."

Purity nodded her head.

***

"See, Erika. That would've been a perfect time for you to tell him." Her sister, Ava told her.

"Don't tell her nothing, Ava. She got herself in this mess so she's going to figure it out by herself. We came here for one thing and that was for her school orientation. She can figure out the rest on her own," her mother said.

"But, Mommy," Ava dragged.

"I don't want to hear it," she said, cutting her off.

Erika was five months pregnant with a little girl and sure enough the baby was Carstin's. Erika found out that she was pregnant a little bit before Carstin decided to move to Baton Rouge, but she didn't know how to tell him. Due to him breaking up with her and leaving her with a broken heart, she knew for a fact that he would think that she was playing games and trying to trap him, but that wasn't the case.

"I'll find a way to tell him. I'm not ready yet." Erika stuffed her cheesecake into her mouth.

"See what I'm saying, Ava?" Her mother shook her head, "How are you not ready to tell this man that you're pregnant with his child when your due date is in less than four months, Erika?"

"I have to find a way to tell him. I never knew we were going to see him tonight, Ma. I was too caught off guard and he was with another woman. That would've been so not classy."

"I wouldn't give a lovely fuck if it was ghetto. You're pregnant with his baby, not her ass," she snapped. "But then again she's probably pregnant too. I told you from the first time I met that boy he wasn't the one for you."

Ava stepped in when she saw her sister eyes watering. "Okay, mommy, calm down."

Their mother was very judgmental and sometimes it became frustrating. Erika wished she would've been like her sister. Ava never allowed her parents to rule their life. If it wasn't for them, Erika would've probably still been with Carstin, living happily ever after. She just allowed them to rule her life too much and because of that she was going through her pregnancy alone, and she was miserable as hell.

"You better tell him before I go to his mama's house and tell her when we get back to Jackson." Her mother poured the sugar into her tea and took a sip.

Erika eyes watered. "That's not your place, Ma."

"But you're my child, and I refuse to sit back and let you raise this baby alone. You didn't make it alone."

"Why is this even the topic of our conversation right now? If we would've never seen Carstin, you wouldn't even be talking about it," Ava said, standing up for her sister.

"But we saw him, so get over it." Brenda rolled her eyes.

"I'm going back to the room. I'll see y'all later." Erika grabbed her purse and waddled out of the restaurant. She cried her entire walk to the car and Ava finally caught up with her.

"Come on, Erika. Don't cry. You know Mama's just trying to look out for you." She rubbed the side of her sister's beautiful, glowing face.

"I'm just so sick of her, Ava. I know that I got myself into this mess, but she's making it no better. First she wants me to handle the shit, but then *she* wants to handle it. I'm just tired of her."

"I know, but you really have to tell him, Erika. If you don't tell him you're going to be a single parent. I keep telling you that Carstin isn't that type of guy. He's going to take care of baby girl regardless."

Erika nodded and wiped her tears.

"You're right." She sniffled. "I just have to think about all of this. I really do."

"And that's okay as long as you tell him."

Erika hugged her sister and kissed her on the cheek. "Thanks for always being understanding. I love you for it.""You've always got my support with whatever you do."

Chapter Nine

The City Bar was crowded with. Paul had the entire club rented for the NBA finals. The seafood and drinks were unlimited. Instead of it being a big club event, Vix and her mother spent their precious time decorating the entire club. One side of the club was decorated in Cavaliers paraphernalia and the other side was decorated with Warriors' décor. It was amazingly beautiful and you would think that some professionals had decorated the place.

The deejay had the music blasting until the game came on and everyone was enjoying themselves. The chefs were already tired and the doors hadn't been open for two hours.

Tarvis and Juice sat at the bar and threw back a few coronas. While Tarvis was checking out which bitch he wanted to take home Juice was staring at the door waiting for one person, Vanity.

"Man, I got to get that bitch standing over there by my auntie," Tarvis said.

"Who that?" Juice asked, slamming down his Corona.

"The one in the red dress. Look at that hoe ass. I bet she can do a few tricks on my dick."

"Old news, man. Been fucked that bitch and her shit is bap and she's stiff."

Tarvis burst out laughing. "Damn, man. Well, just change my mind then."

"Had to keep it real with you, bruh."

"Who you got your eyes on in here tonight?" Tarvis asked, rubbing his hands together.

"Nobody in here." Juice waved the bartender down. "Let me get a shot of Patron."

"What's up with you, man? I don't remember the last time you got you some pussy and all of sudden you acting like you're such a good boy. We do this shit all the time, nigga. Don't tell me one of these thot hoes got your nose wide open?"

Juice chuckled. "Chill out, man. Let's go over here and get on this card table."

Tarvis didn't know what Juice was hiding, but he made a mental note to get to the bottom of it soon.

Vanity and Purity walked through the door and like always all eyes were on them. The server greeted the beautiful ladies with shots of Hennessey. Purity took one and Vanity did too.

"Um, no ma'am." Purity snatched the shot glass from Vanity and drank it and her shot as well.

"Girl, believe me or not, I keep forgetting," Vanity shamefully said.

"Well, you need to remember." She pointed at Juice. "Look who's giving you the death stare."

"Damn, why is he the first nigga I see when we walk in here?" Vanity asked, annoyed.

Purity thought that was funny.

"Oh, there's Carstin. Walk over here with me."

"Okay, but have you talked to Vix?"

Purity shook her head. "Not since earlier."Purity walked through the crowd and Carstin met her. Not caring that people were watching them he grabbed her by her waist and pecked her lips.

Purity was surprised because they had never kissed, but she liked it. Her heart was beating fast, but she enjoyed the feeling. She loved it even more because women that were surrounded around him scattered.

"You smell good, bae," he complimented her.

She winked."You do too, babe."

"What you drinking? I'ma order a bottle so we can go chill alone."

"I can't leave Vanity, though. She's coming too."

"That's cool, come on Vanity," Carstin welcomed her.

"No the fuck I'm not. I'm not about to be third wheeling y'all asses. I'm jealous already," Vanity joked.

"I'ma go ask Paul where Vix is. Y'all love birds enjoy your alone time."

"You sure?" Purity asked.

"Positive."

"Okay. No drinking Vanity."

Carstin ordered a bottle of Hennessey and escorted Purity to his table in the VIP section. For the last two weeks they had been spending a lot of time together. It was almost like they were in a relationship without the title, but Purity loved that he didn't rush her into anything. They took everything one day at a time.

"You kissed me without my permission." Purity giggled.

"I had to. If I would've asked you probably would've told me no."

"Kiss me like that again," she motioned with her finger.

The naughty look on her face made Carstin's dick stand. "Oh yeah?" he excitedly asked. "Yes."

They shared a French kiss that seemed to last forever, and Purity loved it. She didn't want him to stop. Carstin loved the fact that Purity was a rookie. That made him think of Erika when they first started dating. She didn't know a thing, but he taught her everything along the way.

Purity crossed her legs to control what she really wanted him to do to her. She was so ready to experience sex, and if Carstin kept it up, she was definitely going to let him be the first to get a taste of it.

Scene break

When Vanity peeped that Purity was in love with Carstin in their section, she decided to send her a text letting her know that she was about to leave. She couldn't find Vix and she was tired. The swelling around her ankles didn't make it any better. When Purity gave her the okay, she left with Juice on her heels.

"Where are you going?" he asked her.

"I'm going home."

"I'm going with you. Come on."

Vanity looked around to make sure the coast was clear.

"Are you crazy, Juice? Tarvis is going to come out here looking for you. Don't do that."

"Man, come on." He picked her up and carried her to the car. "You shouldn't have come out here anyway."

"Save the speeches for later, Juice."

"Give me kiss."

"No." She turned her head and giggled.

✳✳✳

"Hazel, wait. You're going too deep!" Vix screamed out.

"Hold on, I'm almost done." He stroked harder hitting her spot.

While everyone was at the club partying and celebrating the game, Vix couldn't pass up on a rendezvous with Hazel. Sneaking around with him had turned into something it wasn't supposed to, but Vix loved being with Hazel. There was something about Paul that she couldn't put her finger on, but lately she loved being in Hazel arms more than his. She was surprised that Paul hadn't blown up her phone, but she was glad. She wasn't ready to leave Hazel just yet.

Hazel fell on the side of her and kissed her lips.

"You owe me a massage. I'm going to be sore tomorrow."

He rubbed her thighs. "We ain't done."

"You know I have to get back to the club, Hazel."

"Man, fuck that club. That nigga hasn't even called you."

"But he's going to and after a while he's going to notice that I'm not there by his side. I'm cheating on him remember?"

"Nah, you're cheating on me."

"Hush." She laughed.

"Alright, man. At least let me eat you before you go."

Vix smiled and nodded. "It's waiting on you." She gapped her legs opened. Without hesitation he ate her for a whole hour making her cum back to back.

Once she got herself together she rushed out of the house.

"No kiss?" he asked her.

She ran back on the porch and pecked his lips. She got into her car and sped off not knowing that Sheika was sitting right there in her car with her father taking pictures of everything she had just done.

***

"Fuck!" Tarvis paced the parking lot looking for his wallet and keys. "How the fuck did I slip up like this?" he said, talking to himself.

The minute he talked the honey in the red dress into coming to his house he lost everything. At that moment he knew it was God telling him to let her ass go on. He had lost over a thousand dollars and whoever picked it up had to be a lucky motherfucker.

"So, we're not going to your house?" the lady asked him. She was getting impatient.

"Nah. Call me tomorrow. You got my number."

Luckily for Tarvis, Vix had just pulled up which took him by surprise.

"Where the hell you been all this time?" he asked his sister.

"I had to find something else to wear. I spilled liquor all over my dress," she lied.

"Let me hold your car for tonight. I've lost all my money that I had on me and my keys."

"You can take my car. But what if someone finds your keys and take your car?"

"Damn, you're right. I'ma just go get some more money and my spare from Vanity's house. I'll be back before this shit is over with. Tell the security to make sure my shit don't leave this parking lot."

"Okay. I got you."

The entire drive to Vanity's apartment Tarvis wish he would've listened to Juice and not carry that much money on him in the club. He wasn't broke nor was he hurting, but in his eyes a thousand was too much for a stranger to randomly pick up in the club.

He couldn't wait to talk to Juice. He planned on giving that nigga the cursing of his life for leaving him in the club alone.

He pulled up to Vanity's apartment complex and parked on the side of her. He walked to the door and grabbed the key from under the mat and let himself in.

The apartment was pitch dark how Vanity normally had it.

"Van!" Tarvis called out.

Walking closer toward the room he flinched when he heard moans escaping his little sister's mouth. To say he was disgusted was a complete understatement. He walked toward her dining room and stopped in his tracks when he heard a familiar voice.

"Juice?" he asked himself.

He walked closer to the door and put his ear to it.

"Whose pussy is this, Vanity?" Juice asked, pounding her spot from the side.

"Yours, Juice," she moaned.

Tarvis dropped his head and shook it. If he was a bitch he would've probably shed the tears that threatened to fall from his eyes. But instead he opened the door, causing the two of them to jump.

"Tarvis! What are you doing here?" Vanity asked him in a frightened tone.

"After everything we've been through, this how you repay me, nigga?" Tarvis asked Juice.

Juice shook his head in embarrassment. He wasn't expecting to get caught by anyone and he damn sure didn't want Tarvis to find out like this.

"Aye, bruh, listen…" Juice tried to put on his shirt but was tackled to the floor by an angry Tarvis.

"So you fucking my *sister*, nigga?"

Tarvis punched Juice repeatedly in the face. A part of Juice felt that he deserved it because he knew that Tarvis was hurt, but after reality hit him he lifted Tarvis with all his strength and slammed him to the floor.

Each was aiming to kill the other. It's like all the screaming, begging, and crying that Vanity was doing only made it worse.

"Stop it! Y'all are ruining my house!" She tried to break them up, but was only pushed down.

Paul rushed through the door, breaking them up. "Aye, man, chill out."

"What the hell is going on?" Vix asked, pretending to be lost.

"Your hoe-ass little sister and this fuck nigga right here have been fucking around right under my nose."

"Fuck nigga?" Juice questioned, ready to go for blows again.

"That's what the fuck I said, nigga. You a fuck nigga. I would've never gone behind your back and did no fuck shit like that. But it's cool. Two can play that game." Tarvis went to his hidden spot and got all of his money and belongings.

"You dead to me, Vanity. That's on grandma." He walked out of the house.

"But brother, wait!" Vanity cried out.

"Let him cool off, Vanity. He don't want to hear that right now," Vix told her.

Juice sat on the sofa and stared off into space. Out of all the years that he and Tarvis had known each other, they had never had a falling out or a big fight. Hell, honestly they never really had a disagreement. Juice could see the hurt in Tarvis eyes, but he honestly didn't mean to hurt him. If it wasn't for Vanity, he would've been told him what it was, but due to him trying to respect her and her feelings he had held off.

"Can y'all go to the club and drive his car back to the house? I'm going to take him home." Vix asked her husband.

"It's cool, bae. Go handle that with your brother. I'll have one of my workers drop it off before the night is over with.

When Tarvis first came, Vanity texted Vix and told her what was about to go down her and Paul rushed from the club and headed to the house. Vix was so glad that Vanity had texted when she did because the men had fucked each other up pretty badly.

Vix drove to Tarvis' house in complete silence.

"Are you okay?" Vix looked over and asked her brother.

"Fuck you too, Vix. For real."

"Fuck *me*?" Vix pointed at herself.

"Yeah. Fuck you and fuck Vanity. Don't try to act like you care how I fucking feel because I know you fucking knew. Y'all don't know shit about loyalty, man. That shit kills me. After all the shit I do for y'all and everything I'll do, y'all do some sneaky shit like this behind my back? That's foul. But I got a trick for both of y'all fat asses."

"I'ma just keep my fat-ass mouth closed because I'll fuck you up, little nigga. Don't disrespect me. It wasn't my fucking place to tell you that Vanity and Juice was fucking. The same way you come at me and tell me your secrets, Vanity does too. So no, I wasn't going to tell you what she was doing. She's a grown-ass woman. I'm not fucking him. I'm not pregnant by him, so it ain't my problem," she snapped.

"*Pregnant?*" he yelled, almost piercing her ears.

"Shit," she mumbled. "I'm just saying."

"You just saying what? That fuck nigga got my little sister pregnant?"

"That's not what I said."

"Lie to me so I can slap your ass, Vix. Tonight will be the night your nigga kills me."

Vix didn't respond. She pulled into his driveway and parked the car.

"You're tripping, you're drunk, and you need to calm down before I call Mama over here."

"Mama knows about this shit?"

"No."

"On the real, Vix. I'ma real-ass nigga. It's a lot of shit that I can handle, man, but this right here…I don't know. I can't trust my right-hand man and not even my flesh and blood." His voice cracked. "A nigga feels betrayed in the worst way. That nigga don't deserve my little sister. He a dog-ass nigga."

"Don't downplay Juice, Tarvis. He's not that bad. And to be honest, your little sister ain't a saint either. You know that."

"Fuck all y'all, man. For real!" he yelled. "And ain't no such thing as give me time. I'm done with y'all." He was referring to what she had told Vanity at the house. He got out the car and slammed the door behind him.

Chapter Nine

Chrystal and Willie sat at the dining room table in total shock as they listened closely to what Tarvis was telling them. Words just couldn't define how heartbroken Chrystal was. To hear the things about her baby girl that Tarvis was telling them was quite disturbing. There she was putting her daughter on a pedestal and she pretty much shitted on her and her brother.

"So Vanity and Juice are having an affair?" their father asked him.

"You heard my boy, Willie. You wait until I get my hands on that little sneaky-ass daughter of mine." Chrystal grabbed her phone and continuously tried to call Vanity, but she was ignoring all of them.

"What's so bad about Juice, though?" Willie asked, confused.

"Daddy? Come on, man. My best friend is messing around with my sister?"

"Wouldn't you rather it be him rather than any of these other niggas around here? Shit, I would."

"Juice is a dog, man. He ain't gon' do shit but hurt my sister."

"How do you know Vanity won't hurt him?" he asked.

"What?" Chrystal yelled.

"I've been telling you for the past two years that Vanity wasn't the angel that you thought, baby. Am I surprised about all of this that Tarvis is telling us? Hell no! I mean, he didn't have to do that behind your back, but I would rather him than anyone else. That's just being real. Now, all these other niggas that you're telling us about, I'ma have to talk with my daughter because I won't believe that part."

"I won't make no shit like that up on her."

"Vix, where the hell is your sister?" Chrystal yelled into the phone. "Yeah, that's right. Get y'all sneaky asses over here right now!" she yelled and slammed her phone on the table.

"It's something else I got to tell y'all too."

"Oh, Lord, I don't think I can take anymore. Not right now, son."

"Shit, I want to hear," Willie spoke up.

"Nah, never mind. I'll let Vanity tell y'all. I've said enough."

Little Paul and Jarvis ran into the house and ran straight to their grandmother. It was no other place those two would rather be than there with Chrystal. Vix made sure that her sons had the best bond with their grandma and grandpa, and she loved every minute of it.

"Hey, boys." She kissed their cheeks. "Where's your mammy at?"

"Coming into the house," Little Paul told her, finishing his ice cream.

Vix kissed each boy. "Hey, Mama and Daddy."

"You're not going to speak to your brother?" Chrystal asked.

She shook her head. "I will not. That boy is so disrespectful, Mama. You should've heard how he talked to me last night."

"Y'all disrespectful. Fuck you mean? Don't come in here playing the victim role."

"Boy, get out of your feelings…acting like a little punk. You so disrespectful. Listen at how you're talking in front of Ma and Daddy."

The two of them argued, throwing low blows at one another.

"Hey!" Chrystal yelled. "I don't want to hear that shit. Both of y'all shut your mouths."

Vix grabbed her keys. "I'm about to go," she shot, storming out the house, angrily.

"Where's Vanity?" Willie asked.

She walked in the dining room stuffing her mouth with some greasy chicken fingers from Popeye's. "Here I am Daddy."

Tarvis looked at her and frowned. The fact that she walked into the room unbothered made him want to slap that chicken out of her mouth.

She sat down next to Willie and finished her delicious mashed potatoes.

"You want some, Daddy?" she offered.

"Hell nah. What's this shit your brother telling us about you and Juice?"

She looked at Tarvis. "What did he tell y'all?"

"It don't matter what he told us, what the hell is going on with the two of you, Vanity? You're sleeping with Juice?" Chrystal questioned.

She sighed and used the napkin to wipe her mouth. Even though Vanity was hurt by the entire situation it was nothing she could do but be honest from that point. "The two of us have been seeing each other. Before y'all chew me up and spit me out, I'll admit that I'm wrong for all of this, but I can't change it." Her voice cracked. "I didn't mean for any of this to happen, but it did. I have strong feelings for Juice and it's not like we're just having sex. We have something going."

"Oh, so you and the nigga are in a relationship? I wasn't even respected enough to knowing that much? Tarvis asked.

"It wasn't like that, bro."

He waved her off. "I don't want to hear all that bro shit to be honest."

"Okay, Tarvis, watch your mouth," Chrystal corrected him.

"We're seeing each other, but I don't see what the problem is. It ain't like he dogging me. We spend time together. We like each other. Juice wanted to tell you, but I was scared, so he tried to hold off until I was ready."

"But, Vanity, you and Juice were raised up like cousins. His mama and I are like blood sisters. What the hell is going on here?"

Tarvis shook his head."They just disloyal."

"I don't give a damn about you and Juice. I need to know what the fuck is up with you. Your brother said something about your name ringing bells in these streets. Who all you out here fucking, Vanity?" Willie bluntly asked. "Baton Rouge ain't but so small," he added.

"What?" Vanity's eyes watered as she stared a hole through her brother.

"Why are you crying? Is it true?" Willie asked.

"Wow." She shook her head, and wiped her tears. "So you come and tell them something like that because Juice and I are having an affair? You *that* pressed, nigga?" she asked him.

She was so torn. Yes, she had broken the rules, but she would've never waited until her brother pissed her off to tell his deepest secrets. Then what made it even worse was that he told her parents—who thought the sun set on her.

"That's confirmation right there, Willie." Chrystal stood to her feet and paced the floor. "Lord, I haven't had a drink in years, but this is the day that I'm about to get drunk and pretend none of this has happened." Chrystal cleared her throat.

"That's not all. I have something to tell y'all."

"What?" Willie asked.

"I'm pregnant, and it's Juice's baby."

"You're what, Vanity?" Tears rolled down Chrystal's cheeks.

"I'm sorry, Mama," Vanity cried.

"You wait until your senior year of college to get pregnant by my damn nephew and you don't even have ring on your finger. I'm truly broken right now, Van. Get out of my face before I put my hands on you." She held her chest.

"But, Mama."

"*Out!*" she yelled.

Vanity grabbed her bag of food, and left the house in total disbelief. She knew that they were going to be upset with her, but she didn't know it was going to go that bad.

She got into the car and called Juice.

"What's up, Van?"

"That nigga told my parents everything. They're pissed about everything."

"Damn! Say word?"

"Where are you?"

"Taking my sister to handle some business. I'll be over there soon as drop her off."

"How long will that be?"

"I don't know."

"Well, you need to find out. The fuck?"

"How long do you think we gon' be, Sheika?" he asked his sister. "Give me a, hour, man," he confirmed.

She hung up on him and drove home. She wasn't in the mood to do anything. Not even study for the test she had the next morning.

***

Purity had yet to find a place to live, but she was so comfortable living with her aunt that she had no intention of going back to live with Tawny. Instead of having the bills to worry about she paid the mortgage and the property taxes up for the rest of the year. Work had killed Purity and all she wanted to do was sit in some warm water and Epsom salt and soak her sore bones. Her car was in the shop getting an alignment so Carstin was outside waiting for her. When she got into the car and sighed, he leaned toward her and pecked her soft lips.

"You good?" he asked.

"I'm fine. Just tired. Can you take me to my grandma's house so I can finish packing the rest of my things? My auntie told me I could move everything into the garage until I found somewhere to stay."

"That's cool with me, but let me take you somewhere first," he suggested.

"Where are we going, Carstin? I'm really not in the mood for nothing right now. Today has been rough."

"Chill out. This is gon' make your day better."

Carstin always found Jazz music to be corny as hell, but to ease her mind, he popped in her favorite jazz CD while they rode to the south side of town. She loved that he got to know her in little to no time. That made her feel that he was serious about their relationship.

"You're always doing things that I like, Carstin. Let me hold your phone." He freely handed it to her and she scrolled down his iTunes library list.

"Oh, I like this right here." She clicked on the Yo Gotti and J. Cole song, "Cold Blooded" and turned the volume all the way up.

"You starting to like that hot shit, huh?" He grinned.

She smiled and nodded.

Once they pulled into the house driveway that they had been to a few weeks prior Purity looked a bit upset.

"Aw man, somebody bought it and started fixing it up. I guess you were right when you said it could be fixed, huh?" She poked out her lip at him.

Carstin shook his head because he had purchased the house and started fixing it up for her, but because she didn't catch his drift he played along.

"I told you it could've had some work done, man. I was riding past here earlier and they're hooking this shit the fuck up."

They stepped out of the car and walked up.

"They even put new windows in. It looks fancy."

Purity walked up and peeked inside the window not even noticing that Carstin was opening the door for them to walk in.

She walked behind him. "Carstin, I don't think we're supposed to go inside these people's house."

He smiled and handed both keys to her and then kissed her forehead. "This for you, Ma."

"What?!" she yelled in excitement.

"I wanted to do this for you. I bought you this house. This is what you wanted right?"

Tears welled up in her eyes and her voice cracked. "You didn't have to do this," she said, fumbling around with the key.

He grabbed her head and pecked her cheek. "My girl gets whatever my girl wants. Come on. Let's walk through."

"This house wasn't as bad as we thought it was. I hired a few contractors so they can come in and check the wiring and shit since it's a much older home. I told the painters I wanted this design right here," he pulled out his phone and showed her the interior she had been telling him she wanted for her dream home.

She blushed and that made him happy. Satisfying her was all he wanted to do, and because he had accomplished that, he was feeling like the man.

"Wow. You're so sneaky." She kissed him.

"Nah, I just know how to make some shit shake. I was going to wait until the house was done to show it to you, but I didn't want you to go behind my back and get some other shit. This house will be ready for you to move in, in two months."

"I guess I'm stuck with you now?" She giggled.

"You were stuck with me when we first laid eyes on each other, but I didn't get you this house to hold me and you over your head. I got you this because I'm feeling you. I want this to be more than just boyfriend and girlfriend someday, and you're a good person. You really deserve to be treated with the finer things."

"Aww..." She hugged him. "You're sweet, Carstin."

"I like the sound of bae better than Carstin," he joked.

"Sorry, bae. But before we get deeper, I need to meet your mom. That'll let me know this real."

"Whenever you're ready to take the trip, it's on."

Purity nodded and smiled as they walked back to the car. She couldn't wait to get home and tell her auntie about all of it. She still couldn't believe that he had gone all out of his way to buy her a home. Her mind immediately flooded with all the harsh and nasty things Tawny used to say to her. Was it real? She wondered.

Chapter Ten

"I just don't know, baby," Chrystal told her husband. "I can't believe that Vanity is pregnant by Juice, but I did think about what you told me and I love Juice. That's my boy, and he's good for her. I think it broke my heart more that she hurt her brother, though."

Chrystal was under the impression that Willie was taking her to Chili's for her birthday since that's what she had been wanting for the last two days, but the girls were at her store preparing for her big surprise party that Vanity had planned. Vanity and Chrystal were always considered best friends and the fact that Chrystal had shut her out, was breaking her heart. She had to do something to fix it. Willie was in charge to waste time until the party started at five o'clock and it was almost that time.

"Bingo! I kept telling your ass that was your problem. You hated to see Tarvis hurt so you got mad with my baby."

"You were mad with your baby too. Don't put it all on me."

"Yeah, but not about Juice. I don't think it's right that you've been ignoring her. She needs you more now than ever, especially since she's pregnant. Tarvis is a grown-ass man. I bet you any amount of money he'll fuck Sheika behind Juice's back."

"Willie!"

"What? Shit, I'm just saying."

She laughed and looked out the window. "Your mouth has always been filthy. I don't know how we connected."

"We connected because we love each other."

When Willie parked at Chrystal's pharmacy she was a bit confused. "What the hell? You said we were going out for food," she argued.

"I left my briefcase here last night on your desk. Come on."

"I'll wait for you in the car, babe. My feet hurt."

"Man, bring your lazy ass on. Those heels are two inches. I don't have my key to the place."

She rolled her neck, then sighed and got out. "I would think it's your birthday today instead of mine."

She placed the key into the door lock and pushed it open for him. When the lights turned on and everyone jumped out screaming, "Surprise!" she almost had a heart attack. She never saw that one coming.

"Oh my God!" She smiled so bright. "Willie!" She hit him in the arm and kissed him.

"Happy Birthday, baby. It was Vanity's idea," he told her.

She took a look around and couldn't believe her eyes. The place was so beautiful and it was jammed pack with family, friends, and shoppers that usually came to the store. It was no secret that Chrystal was loved in the community, but they had overdone themselves with the party. The food table was overflowing with all kinds of barbecue, delicious sides, and desserts. She felt even more grateful that Vix, Vanity, and Purity were humble enough to be the servers. They wore their hats and Chrystal's pharmacy aprons.

Vanity handed her the gift she had purchased for her and kissed her on the cheek. "Happy birthday, Mama."

"Thank you, baby. I love you. We'll talk after all of this."

Vanity nodded. "Enjoy yourself. Ms. Sonya had to run back to her house because stupid-ass Juice forgot to put your gift in the back seat like she told him to."

"A gift? Sonya ain't have to get me no gift. None of y'all had to."

"Cut it out, Auntie. You deserve all of this." Purity danced around.

"Lord, y'all done turned my niece out already," Chrystal said, causing everyone to laugh.

Tawny walked up with her drink. "Happy birthday, Chrystal."

"Thank you, baby sister."

"I need to speak with you after the party's over, missy," Tawny told Purity.

"Okay," Purity said just before walking off.

Paul, Carstin, Juice and all the other men were behind the building shooting dice. They allowed all the women to have fun on the inside while they enjoyed themselves out back.

Vix and Vanity were sitting at the table relaxing. They had been at the store since eight o'clock that morning cooking and decorating. It felt good to see that big beautiful smile spread across Chrystal's face when she walked in. They had done everything they needed to do.

"I want to see Hazel so bad," Vix told her sister.

"Well, you must've known he was coming because there he is right there." Vanity pointed.

When Vix turned around and saw Hazel and some of his men walk through the door, she wanted to piss on herself. Chrystal had always loved Hazel. She wasn't sure if he was coming to start some shit with Paul or if he was coming to show love to her mother. She thought he would've been perfect for Vix if she wasn't married.

Vix wanted to walk over to him and beg him to leave, but she knew better than to approach him while Paul was not too far from them. She sat there and stared at him, begging him not to start anything with her pleading eyes. He winked and nodded his head, assuring her that everything was going to be alright.

He walked over to the gift table and placed all of the gifts he'd gotten Chrystal on it.

"Hey, baby! How are you?" Chrystal hugged him and he kissed her cheek.

"I'm good, Ma. I heard about your big surprise party and I couldn't miss bringing you something special."

"You didn't have to do that, Hazel. Did you see Vix them over there?"

"Yes, ma'am. I saw her. I don't want to go over there, though. You know how her husband can get." He giggled.

Chrystal rolled her eyes. She couldn't stand Paul.

"Yeah, I know. At least wave."

Hazel waved and blew a kiss, causing Vix to blush. Only if Chrystal knew that they saw each other every day.

Paul and Carstin walked back into the store and Paul had to take a double look.

"What the fuck?" he said.

"What's up, bruh?" Carstin asked.

"That's the nigga, Hazel, that I told you about."

"Oh, okay. But what made the nigga show up?" Carstin asked, confused.

"That's what I'm 'bout to see," he said, walking over to where Chrystal and Hazel were and joined the conversation.

He kissed her cheek. "What's up, Ma?"

"Hey, Paul. Hazel just came by to bring me a gift."

"What's up, Hazel?" Paul greeted.

Hazel gave him a head nod, which offended him.

Hazel smiled at her ignoring that Paul was still standing there. "I'll see you later, Ms. Chrystal."

"You don't want to take a plate, baby?" she asked him.

"No, ma'am. I'm good."

"Okay, well don't be a stranger. Take care. Thanks for the gift."

"No problem," he said, before leaving the building.

When Hazel left, Vix let out a sigh of relief.

"That was close as fuck," Vanity whispered.

Vix threw her drink back. "I know, right?"

"Let me holler at you for a minute, Vix," Paul calmly said.

The two of them walked into the kitchen. Once Vix closed the door Paul snapped. "Why the fuck does that nigga feel comfortable popping up at your mama's party? You invited him?"

"No. Is that even a real fucking question? We told everyone in the community about the surprise party. Why would I need to tell Hazel?"

"Maybe Vanity's messy ass told him."

"Aye, nigga, chill on my sister. Vanity don't talk to Hazel, and she wouldn't do that. All he did was bring her a fucking gift and left. I don't talk to him and I haven't talked to him in forever. You're tripping."

"I better be only fucking tripping."

She rolled her eyes and left him standing there feeling insecure and foolish.

"Damn, I'm tripping," he said to himself.

Carstin walked in. "Cheating will make you wonder, nigga."

"Shut the fuck up, nigga."

Meanwhile, while everyone was on the inside partying and having a good time Purity walked outside where her mother and Tarvis were. They were passing a blunt back and forth.

"Hey, Tawny. What you wanted to talk about?" she asked her.

She handed him the blunt. "Give us a minute, Tarvis."

"Nah, you can finish that, Auntie. I'm 'bout to go in here and eat."

"I have to talk to you about something important."

"Okay, what's up?" Purity nursed her drink.

"Well, last month a little lump formed under my arm. At first I thought it was a little cyst so I went to the doctor to have him take a look at it. They ran a few tests on me and when the results came back they saw cancer."

"What?" Purity asked, almost choking on her liquor. "Cancer? What? How?" she asked on the verge of tears.

Tawny wiped the tears the spilled down her cheeks. "Aretha's ass cursed me with this cancer shit."

"What? Grandma didn't even have cancer. Don't start that, Tawny. Now ain't the time."

"Wrong. She *did* have cancer. She just hid it from you."

Purity stood there in shock. Tawny was telling her too much at one time. She couldn't deal with it.

"How bad is the cancer?"

"It started under my arm and has spread down to right breast. It's bad. I'm telling you because I need you to handle all my medical bills so that I can get my treatments."

Tears fell from Purity eyes. "Is that the only reason you told me? Because you need me to cover your expenses?"

"Purity, if you don't help me I'ma die."

"But, Mama, do you hear yourself? You just said you only told me because you need me to pay for medical bills."

Tawny was taken back because that was the first time in a long time that Purity had actually called her *Mama.*

Aggravated, Purity stormed off, "I just can't take this." "Purity!" Tawny called out for her.

When Purity walked inside she went to the back and grabbed her belongings. She was crying so bad that everyone noticed. Chrystal was pissed because she knew it had to be Tawny's ass.

"Bae? What's wrong?" Carstin asked her.

"Just take me away from here, Carstin," she told him.

He nodded and grabbed her hand.

"Wait, P, what's wrong with you?" Vix asked.

"Tawny's ass."

"I fucking knew it. Where's her ass at?" Chrystal stormed out front.

"What did you do, Tawny? You're always starting some shit with that girl," she snapped.

Tawny giggled. "Not my Christian sister, cursing. Arethamust be having a fit in heaven." She drank the rest of her liquor, "What me and Purity talk about is my business. That's my child. Not yours," she slurred.

"Tarvis take your auntie home, will you?"

"Yes, ma'am."

"I can walk myself," she said, snatching away from Travis. "I ain't that drunk."

He shook his head and got into his car. He didn't know what to say about Tawny and her evil ways.

Chapter Eleven

Tarvis walked out of the Circle K eating his Skittles and drinking his Mountain Dew voltage drink. He slowly walked to his car and tried to watch the man beating the woman's ass at the same time. He would've helped, but shit was so crazy around his way, he didn't want to involve himself in anything that he didn't know about.

"Stop fucking with me, Sheika! For real!"

When Tarvis heard JT's loud harsh voice he tossed the Skittles and drink and ran over toward them. When he saw Sheika sitting on the curb holding her bloody nose and busted lip, Tarvis grew furious.

"Man, what the fuck, Sheika?! What's good?! Why you letting this nigga do you like this?!" Tarvis asked, giving her a hand.

"Don't fucking worry about her, nigga!" JT yelled before he lit up a cigarette.

"I'm okay, Tarvis. Don't get in trouble behind me, seriously," Sheika cried.

Tarvis pulled her to the car and opened the passenger's door.

"Sit right here and don't move. I'll be right back."

He went to his side of the car and reached for his gun under his seat. Sheika was so busy crying and holding her face that she didn't even notice that Tarvis had the gun. He walked back over to where JT was and hit him in the eye with the gun causing him to stumble.

When JT was down on the ground Tarvis pistol whipped him until his face was covered in blood.

"You think this shit is a game nigga?" Tarvis asked, stomping JT out.

"You need to leave before I call the police." The store employee came out and said.

Sheika was watching everything from the car, but she wouldn't move. She didn't want to stop Tarvis because she was tired of the way JT treated her and abused her. She had done nothing to deserve the treatment he dished out to her and she had finally learned her lesson. JT didn't give a damn about her. All he wanted her to do was leave him the fuck alone.

Tarvis got into the car and pulled off. "You got to stop letting that nigga do you like that, Sheika. Look at your fucking face, man," Tarvis argued."I know," Sheika cried. "I finally get the picture."

"That nigga has always been a bitch made nigga…slapping women around and shit just to feel good. That shit ain't what's up, man. But I bet you he won't fuck with you no more."

"He and Juice just had it out at Mama's house a while ago. They don't even know that I'm still messing around with him."

"Yeah?"

"Yes. Don't tell them about this okay?" She looked into her purse for some napkins. "Where are you going? My house is the other way."

"You going to my house tonight, shit. I ain't driving all the way back to the hood tonight."

"I don't have anything to wear, though."

"It's cool. I'll give you some ballers and a t-shirt. You can sleep in the guest room downstairs."

"Thank you. You ain't have to do that."

"Charge that shit to the game. You family."

"You still mad with my brother?" she asked him.

"I ain't mad, but I don't fuck with him," Tarvis fronted.

Sheika giggled. As long as she could remember those two were brothers. Blood couldn't make them any closer. Sheika thought that both of them were being completely ridiculous.

"Get out your feelings, Tarvis. He and Vanity's fat ass make a cute couple. Don't front."

"Girl, don't call my baby fat. They don't make shit."

"I've been calling Vanity my little fat baby since she was little. She's a pretty thick one. And one thing I always knew about her ass was that she didn't give a lovely fuck about her weight. She dresses better than me, and you know I got all the style."

Tarvis chuckled and thought. Maybe he was being a bitch-ass nigga. He knew that he was wrong for telling his parents about how Vanity had been acting in the streets, but he knew that she wasn't going to slow down until they sat down and had a real talk with her.

"You think I'm tripping?" Tarvis asked.

"I do. If they love each other, let them be. Both of them are grown."

"You know Vanity's pregnant?"

"*What*?!" Sheika yelled.

"Sonya ain't tell you? Van is pregnant by that nigga."

"Oh my God, No! I'm going to be an auntie? I wonder why the fuck they didn't tell me."

"I don't know, but yeah. You're going to be an auntie, and I'm going to be a damn uncle. I can't believe Vanity's hot ass is going to have one before me."

"Have you one, then."

"Hell nah. These bitches ain't shit. They aint 'bout to trap a young nigga like me. Besides, I'm not ready for kids. My life ain't in order for that shit."

"All women ain't bad. You're just used to messing with those trashy little sluts from the south side. Get you a real woman. Go sit your ass in church with your mama one Sunday and find you one. It's some good ones left."

"The *church*? Where you think all my hoes go every Sunday? Those hoes from the south side ain't the worst. It's the school girls and the church girls who are," Tarvis said, making Sheika double over in loud laughter.

When they pulled up to the house, Tarvis got out and Sheika was right behind him. He walked into the house and flicked on the lights.

"Damn, man, it's cold as fuck in here, and you're messy as shit, Tarvis. When's the last time you cleaned up in this big-ass house?"

"I don't clean. Vanity usually does it for me."

"Well, I'll sure as hell clean for you before I shower. This is ridiculous."

He laughed. "Shut up and come in here. Let me nurse your bloody face."

She followed him to the living room and got comfortable on the couch. At least he had the decency to keep the front room clean.

Chapter Twelve

Chrystal and Sonya walked into Chrystal's house after having a long day. Chrystal was very upset in the beginning about Vanity's pregnancy, but after going to Vanity's doctor's appointment with her and Juice earlier that day, the two mothers were happy as ever.

Chrystal heard Purity and Carstin's voice coming from her room so she decided to walk back there and see what they had going on.

"Hey, Auntie," Purity spoke sadly.

"Hey, baby. Where you going?" Chrystal asked.

Purity had outfits spread over the bed along with a big suitcase.

"We're going to see my mama this weekend, Ms. Chrystal. I don't know why she's packing like we're leaving for a year. I told her I would take her shopping when we got there anyway," Carstin told her.

"I just want to make sure that all my clothes are presentable. What's so bad about that?" Purity asked Carstin.

He threw his hands up in surrender.

"Carstin, let me talk to Purity for a minute please."

"Yes, ma'am. I'll be in my car, P. I have to make a few calls about your house anyway."

Chrystal closed the door behind him and sat on the bed with Purity.

Chrystal pat Purity's thigh. "I see the hurt in your eyes. Talk to me."

Purity burst into tears. "I'm broken. Tawny really has cancer, Auntie. She wasn't lying about it."

Chrystal eyes filled with tears. She shook her head. "Lord, Jesus! I am so sorry, baby."

"I don't know what to do. My easy-going spirit will not allow me to turn my back on Tawny. I know that she's evil and she can be mean, but she has cancer. I never saw Tawny cry so hard before in my life."

"You must've gone with her to the doctor?"

Purity nodded her head. "Yes. I went with her because I thought she was lying to get the money. It's really bad, though, Auntie. The cancer has spread so badly."

Chrystal wiped her tears that fell from her eyes. She thought that Tawny was lying too, but to find out that she really had cancer made her heart sink to the pit of her stomach. Aretha had suffered from cancer plenty of times, but she never thought that her big sister would go through the same thing. Chrystal was exactly how Purity was—easy-going. She refused to let her sister go through it alone.

"I am so sorry, baby." Chrystal hugged Purity tight. "Don't you worry about your mama. I'm going to make sure that she's fine. You don't have to spend a dime of your money. Do you hear me? I'll handle all of that. You go out of town and enjoy yourself."

"I can't even think about having fun with Carstin, Auntie Chrystal. I'm worried sick about my mama."

"Listen at me, P. Whether you know it or not, you have a good-ass man outside. Now I don't know much about Carstin, but since he's been around here, I must say that he's shown himself to be a good young man. Haven't you been wanting a man like him? Ain't that what you've always told me?"

"Yes, ma'am. I just feel like he came into my life at the wrong time. I'm not stable enough to love someone."

"Yes, you are. Go meet his mama. I would tell you to have sex, but if you can wait, I want you to wait." They both laughed, "Seriously. I'ma go around here and check on your mama. You just go and enjoy yourself, okay?"

Purity smiled and nodded her head. She was so thankful that she had her auntie to keep her sane at a time like this She was truly lost and confused. Although she did love the way Carstin had stepped in and proved that he was the one, she never wanted him to be able to say that she wasn't a good enough girlfriend. She knew that it would've been super easy to let go so she wasn't. If he really wanted something with her he would have to accept it all… her crazy-ass mama and her crazy ass life too.

***

Paul, Vix, Little Paul, and Jarvis sat at the dinner table. Vix was beyond pissed that Paul's phone continuously rang off the hook while Little Paul was saying the grace over their dinner.

Little Paul closed out the prayer."God bless the food and God bless Mommy and Daddy. Amen."

"Amen, Mommy's big boy." Vix leaned over and shook his jaws from side to side.

"Let me take this call for a minute, baby." Paul excused himself from the table.

Vix was so disgusted, and Paul didn't even know that he was giving her every reason to fall back in love with Hazel. Lately, their communication had been awful and what made it even worse was he stayed out of town at least three times every two weeks. Vix was tired and definitely at her breaking point in their marriage. He barely had time to fuck her, which wasn't a problem because she was getting that from Hazel every chance she got. But it made shit so much harder to keep giving Hazel the marriage excuse. If she hadn't put so much time into their marriage she would've served him the divorce papers by now, but the love she had for him just wouldn't allow her to do it.

"Nah, hell nah, I can come out there tonight if you want me too, boss. You know that ain't a problem," Paul spoke into the phone.

Vix shook her head and rolled her eyes in pure disgust. She finished up the side salad that she had fixed herself and wrapped her homemade lasagna up. She grabbed her phone and texted Purity and Vanity in their group message: Vix: I think I'm ready for a divorce ☹

Vanity: Damn, Hazel's dick game is that serious? This nigga got you ready to leave Paul?"

Purity: LMAO! What Vanity said. Vix, you can't leave your husband. Remember what you and Hazel are doing is just fun.

Vix: I'll call y'all on my way out. Don't text back.

Vanity: Love you. Don't forget. OK?

Vix deleted every message so she wouldn't have any evidence on her.

"Baby, don't be mad, but I got to fly back out to Jamaica. Some serious work came in, and I need to get that while I can."

Vix waved him off. "Chile, go on, Paul."

"What the fuck are you tripping for?" He frowned.

"Come on, Paul. Don't do that in front of the boys. Go pack your bags and go on to Jamaica. Bye."

"We're done, Mama," Little Paul informed her, kicking his legs back and forth.

Paul frowned at him. "So go wash you and your little brother up."

"Nah, I'll wash them up. What do you mean?"

"Man, you got to stop spoiling those boys. I brought them a stool to step on. He's big enough to get it."

"Boy, you got me fucked up! My baby ain't big enough to be stepping on that stool to hold Jarvis so he can clean him up. Are you dumb or are you dumb as fuck? He can hurt the both of them."

"Nah, but I think your ass is dumb talking to me like you motherfucking crazy!" He raised his voice, causing Jarvis cry.

"Boy, you just don't know," Vix laughed. She shook her head, thinking how she wanted to let his ass know that all that power he once had was almost gone.

"I must don't know what?"

She ignored him and picked Jarvis up. "Come on, baby. Let's get y'all washed up before y'all go to Mama house," she told Little Paul."What's up with you lately, Vix? Every day I come home, you're mad. Tell me what's up, Ma," he asked her, almost begging.

"What's up with me lately or what's up with *you*, Paul?" Vix yelled on the verge of tears, "Since when did you let money rule our entire marriage. You're gone so much that I barely see you now, and when we do spend time, your fucking connect, and whoever else, is interrupting us. You couldn't even answer that phone and tell them that you were having dinner with your family. You got shit fucked up. This isn't how it should be!" she yelled, fed up.

He pecked her lips. "I'm sorry, baby. But all this shit I'm doing is for *us*. It'll be over soon, okay?"

"I hear you. When are you leaving?"

"I'ma leave in about two more hours. I'll be back in two days, alright?"

"How come you never ask me to go with you to your meetings?" she asked, catching him off guard.

"I don't want you around that shit anymore."

She chuckled and pushed him out of the way.

"Be safe on your trip." She washed the boys up, leaving him there looking stupid.

***

Vix jumped into Hazel's arms as soon as he opened the door. She wrapped her big thighs around his waist and placed kisses all over his face.

"Damn, woman, hold up!" he laughed.

She smothered him with more kisses. "I've missed you."

He looked into her eyes and smiled. "That nigga went out of town again?" he asked her.

"Yes. But at least I get to be with you for two days."

"Yeah, I love that shit." He smiled and put her down. "Let me get your bags."

She walked into the kitchen and hopped up on the counter. She loved being with Hazel so much that it was almost scary. She hadn't seen him since Chrystal's party and she was in need of some of his good loving.

He walked between her thighs and slipped his tongue into her mouth. She threw her hands around his neck and scooted to the edge of the counter.

He stepped back and grabbed her hand and noticed that she had taken off her ring.

"Where your ring?" he asked.

She shrugged. "I don't like the way you look at it so I took it off."

"Nah, what are you and that nigga going through? And don't lie either."

She sighed and crossed her arms over her chest. "He's never home anymore. He leaves the fucking country more than Obama, and it's annoying. I know that I'm tripping because I'm the one who's cheating on him, but I think he's cheating too. I could be tripping, but I feel it in my gut. There's no way he has to go out of town that much for dope."

Vix knew she had no business pillow talking about her marriage, but she knew that everything she talked about was safe right there with Hazel. He kissed her neck. "I don't know what he's doing, but I know he's fucking up by letting me get you how I want you."

"I have to tell you something, Hazel." She cleared her throat.

"Tell me anything." He opened the refrigerator and poured himself a glass of water.

Stuttering, she said, "I'm pregnant a-a-and it's y-y-yours."

Hazel's eyes widened and a large lump formed in his throat. "Say you swear, Vix."

"I swear. I added up the dates, and it's yours. I wouldn't lie to you about something so serious. If it was Paul's, you know I'd tell you."

"Vix, I swear if you tell me you're gon' kill my baby, just leave now, bruh. For real."

"Calm down. I won't do that to you. I know how much the last baby hurt you. I must be honest with you and tell you that I don't know what the fuck I'm going to do. I'm pregnant with your child and I'm married to another man. Paul will kill us both."

"I don't give a fuck about that nigga. I'll kill his ass first," Hazel spat.

"What should I do?"

"Don't let him find out right now. We'll think of something." Hazel pulled at his beard. "I got something to tell you too, though."

Vix frowned. "Please don't tell me you got another bitch, man?"

"Nah, I'm telling you that you need to prepare to leave that nigga. I've been patient long enough. You ain't in love with that nigga, man."

"Don't rush me. Let me figure some shit out."

"How long you talking?" he asked caressing her stomach.

"Just a few more weeks I need to see what's up with him."

Hazel pulled her shirt over her head, bent down, and kissed her stomach. To say that he was the happiest man on earth was a complete understatement. He was going to have a baby with Vix and she finally understood how much he loved her. Even though she had her suspicions about her husband cheating, she still felt bad that she was preparing to leave him. She knew that Paul wasn't going to stop anytime soon and he had his reasons to why he was traveling so much.

"Take off these tight ass shorts. You're probably choking my baby's head." He tugged at her pants.

She laughed loud. "Shut up fool. It's only a little egg inside of me."

The both of them laughed.

She jumped down from the counter and followed him into the living room. They normally would've rushed into sex, especially after not seeing each other in two weeks. Hazel was excited about Vix being pregnant but he was more worried than excited. He didn't want Vix to be in danger with Paul and he had to think of a master plan to get her from under that nigga.

"What's on your mind, baby?" Vix asked him.

"I just don't want shit to go bad. You can't let him find out you pregnant with my seed until you leave him, okay?"

She laughed. "No worries, Hazel. I love my life more than you know."

Hazel didn't crack a smile. He was serious. If something was to happen to her or his unborn seed he would go crazy. The faster she left the nigga the better it would've been though.

Hazel pulled at his beard. "You know what I was thinking? How 'bout you and I go on a cruise or some shit? Lets' leave for a vacation for about a week? I get tired of being cooped up in this damn house. If a nigga can't show you off around here, you might as well let me take you away from here."

"Hell nah. Paul wouldn't go for that. Me? Leaving the country? That man knows me like a book. Now, if my sister and them could go with me, we could make it look like it was a girls trip."

He caressed her thighs. "Tell them to come with us then. Vanity wouldn't mind. Everything's on me."

"They wouldn't be comfortable, Hazel. It's going to be me and you and just them."

"Man, those girls won't be worried about our asses, man. Just shoot them a text and ask. If they say no, I won't pressure you anymore."

"Okay." Vix grabbed her phone from her purse and sent out a text.

Vix: I need a favor y'all... Hazel wants to take me on a cruise and I know Paul won't believe that I'm going without a man unless y'all come with me. Can y'all come just to cover for me? Hazel's paying for everything.

Vanity: Hell fuck yeah, I'll go! I need a vacation after these finals anyways. When are we leaving?

Purity: Vix is trying to get all of us killed. I'll go as long as it's after I come back from Jackson next week.

Vix: OMG! Thank y'all! I thought y'all would say no. So y'all won't feel bad that me and Hazel will be the only couple?

Vanity: Nope!

Vix smiled, showing off of her beautiful teeth.

"What they say?" Hazel asked.

She shrugged and kissed his lips. "They said yes, baby. My sister said she needs a vacation."

"It's wherever you want to go, princess." He stuck his tongue into her mouth and they shared the longest kiss ever.

"I don't know how we fell for each other so fast, but I love it. If loving your ass is wrong, I swear don't want to be right."

"We were already in love. We just reconnected."

He tickled her on her neck and they ran around the house playing like kids. That's what love meant to Vix.

Chapter Thirteen

It was Purity's second day in Jackson, Mississippi with Carstin and his family, and she was enjoying herself. Carstin's mother, Claudia, made Purity feel very comfortable, but she was still trying to adjust to the rest of the family. It took Purity no time to realize that Carstin was crazy about his family. Everyone loved him, and they spoke so highly of him.

"You want anything else to eat, Purity?" Claudia asked.

"No, ma'am, I'm okay. Thank you." Purity smiled.

"Okay, come help me in the kitchen. Let's have some girl talk."

Claudia and her husband, Richard, were having a family cookout in their yard, and the yard was jammed pack. Carstin was on the other side wetting the kids with the water hose and throwing them in the pool. They were having a blast. Claudia placed the dishes into the dish water. "I'm so happy my son finally found him a good young lady. You have no idea."

"Aw, Ms. Claudia, that's so sweet. Thank you."

"I knew you were a good one when he said you weren't trying to go further until you met me. That's what I like; self-respect."

"Oh yes, if my grandmother never taught me anything, she always taught me self-respect," Purity assured her.

"Tell me this. You speak so highly about your grandmother and not your mom. Why?"

"My grandma raised me, and we were much closer than my mom and I are."

"I understand. Believe it or not, that's exactly how my grandma and I were. We were closer than my mama and me." Claudia shook her head. "I'll give my life to have my grandma back."

Purity shook her head. "Tell me about it."

"P, are you good?" Carstin came behind her and gripped her waist and kissed her cheek.

She laughed. "Yes, babe. I'm fine. You're really wet, though."

He sighed and sat down. "Yeah, I know. My little cousins know exactly how to work a nigga."

"I put your plate in the microwave, baby," Claudia told Carstin.

"Appreciate it, Mama." He went into his old room to change his clothes. Once he changed he walked back into the kitchen.

"You ready?" he asked Purity.

She nodded her head. "I'm ready if you are."

"Why are you leaving so soon, son?" Claudia asked.

"I got a meeting in the morning at the store. A big shipment of tile and carpet is supposed to be coming in, and I want to see how my team is handling things."

Purity smiled. She was so impressed.

"That's alright with me, son. I'm so proud of you. I don't know if I tell you that enough."

"And I appreciate you for it, Mama."

"Come by tomorrow, will you? I'll prepare a dinner for you, Purity, and Richard. It'll be like a double date."

"That sounds good, Ms. Claudia. I'd love that."

After gathering their things, they headed to Carstin's house. It was a three bedroom, two bathroom house, but it was beautiful and big enough just for him. It didn't take a blind man to know that a woman had decorated his house, and Purity knew that woman was his mother. His house's décor was so much similar to his mother's. He just had more men's stuff.

Purity sat on his lap. "I'm really enjoying myself, babe."

"Yeah, your ass is loosening up a lot too." He laughed and kissed her.

"Um, Carstin, I, um," she stuttered.

"Say what you got to say, P. You ain't got to be scared to talk to me."

"I'm ready for you to make love to me," she said, looking into his eyes.

"Yeah?" He smiled.

"Yes. I'm ready. But, Carstin, you have to understand that once I give you my virginity, you'll have a very important piece of me. You've given me every reason to trust you, and I'm falling in love with you more and more. Please don't give me a reason to regret my decision."

"You don't have to worry about me hurting you, P. That's something I will *never* do." He kissed her neck and she threw her head back and enjoyed the tingling feeling that went through her body.

She was on fire and she was ready to finally experience lovemaking. She didn't know the first thing to do in the bedroom, but she did remember a lot of things from watching porn. She hoped that she could deliver what those girls on the flicks delivered. She didn't want to turn him off and be boring.

When they got into the bedroom she slowly took off her long sundress and exposed her flawless body. Carstin's dick rose just at the sight of it. The glimpse he'd gotten when he walked in on her when she was showering was nothing compared to now. Her thighs were big, but she was shaped like a goddess. Her fat ass sat out so perfectly. Her breasts weren't that big, but they fit perfectly with her shape. Carstin slung his tank top to the side of the bed, along with his Levi's jeans. He hadn't had sex since the two of them had been dealing with each other, so was ready to wear her ass out.

He pulled her in close to him and released her from her bra. He gently bit down on her right nipple and licked on it in circular motion.

"Mmm…" she moaned.

"Lay back on the bed," he instructed her.

She did as she was told and opened her legs wide. He got on both knees and pulled her to the edge. Once he slid her panties down he ate her like she was his last meal.

"Oh my God, Carstin!" Purity screamed out.

He took one finger and stuck it into her tight, juicy, honey pot. He had no idea how he was going to fit inside of her without hurting her, but he was going to make it work.

He flicked her clit back and forth with his thick tongue.

"I think I'm going to cum, bae!" she screamed and released a much-needed orgasm. That didn't make him stop pleasing her orally, though. He sucked on her clit until she had tears escaping her eyes. The feeling was unexplainable.

Once he whipped his long thick dick out she wanted to scream, but they were too caught up in the moment to back out.

"What you want me to do now?" she asked him.

"Lay back down and spread your legs. I got it," he told her.

He gently pushed himself inside of her, trying his best not to hurt her. The feeling of her tight lips wrapping around his manhood almost made him cum instantly. Even Erika's pussy wasn't that good when he took her virginity.

"Shit," Purity bit down on her knuckle.

"Let me know if you can't take it, P. I'll stop," he told her.

She grabbed the back of his arms. "Keep going."

"Fuck," he moaned with a thrust. "You're wet as fuck, P." He leaned down and kissed her.

The pain went away after a few strokes. Carstin was impressed when Purity was grinding with him. They were enjoying it and didn't want it to end.

Purity closed her eyes tight. "That's my spot, Carstin. Oh, shit, and I'm about to cum again!" she screamed.

He rubbed her clit in circular motion with his thumb. She couldn't believe it. She was grateful that her first time was with someone so experienced and who knew how to please her. Carstin was the truth in her eyes and fucking him every chance she got was a must.

"I want to ride it," Purity told him.

"You think you can handle that?" he asked her, seriously.

She nodded her head. She would do anything that Carstin wanted to do. She loved the fact that the entire time he made it about her. He only did things she was comfortable with doing and because of that, she wanted to return the favor.

When he laid back he wasn't expecting her to go down on him, but he damn sure wasn't going to stop her.

When her plump juicy lips wrapped around his dick he jerked. He watched his dick disappear a few times in her mouth and he was impressed. Even though it was her first time in bed, she sure knew how to fuck, and she could suck dick too. Her head bobbed up and down and she massaged his balls making him moan a little.

"Shit, girl," he moaned, biting down on his bottom lip.

"You like it?" she asked.

He nodded his head and closed his eyes. When she climbed back on him and slowly lowered herself onto his shaft, she let out a loud scream. It didn't hurt at all. In fact, it felt better than him being on top. He gripped her ass and slowly grinded into her. He knew that she was going to make him bust being in that position, so he had to be in control.

She slowly bounced on him making her ass clap.

"Aw, shit, P. I'm 'bout to bust!" he screamed out, "Get up."

He didn't have to tell her twice, P hopped off of him with the quickness. She watched the cum oozed out the tip of his dick and decided to clean it up with her mouth. Sucking him back hard, they went at it a few more times that night before they were both tired.

Never in a million years did she think her first time would be that good. She had heard so many horror stories about how the first time was the worst, but she couldn't agree less. It was the best and she was glad that Carstin was the one to give it to her. She knew for a fact that she was in love with him after that.

While he slept peacefully, she did what Vix had told her to do and soaked in the tub to ease her bones so they wouldn't hurt the next morning. She had been texting Vanity and Vix telling them about her first time and they seemed more hyped than her. It was beyond funny and exciting. She could finally have sex talk with them without feeling like the odd girl out.

Chapter Fourteen

Paul sat in his last meeting before he would have to leave and go back home. A two-day trip had turned into a three-day trip, and he wasn't feeling it at all. Melissa got more aggravating by the day, and he would rather be home with his wife and kids making shit right. He hated that he and Vix's relationship was going back to how it was in the beginning, so he was more determined to fix things at home.

Melissa's father sat at the head of the table and broke down the process of their new shipments and how they'd be coming in. When Don mentioned that Paul and his men would have to come to Jamaica five times a month for the rest of the year, he let out a sigh of frustration. He knew that wasn't going to work, especially with Vix already being fed up.

"Is everything clear?" Don asked everyone in the meeting.

Paul wasn't happy at all and wanted to say 'Hell fuck nah! My wife ain't on this shit!' but he knew better than to disrespect Melissa in front of her father.

"Everything is clear," Paul spoke up.

"Okay. I need everyone out the conference room except my daughter, Paul, ad me. Thanks y'all. Next meeting is in two weeks at the same time."

Everyone got up and left. Paul wasn't sure what they needed to talk about, but he was ready for him to say whatever he had to say so he could get on his plane and head out.

Paul adjusted his tie. "What's up, boss man?"

"My daughter has something she wants to tell you and she would rather say it in front of me," Don said.

"What's up, Melissa?"

When she dropped her head, Paul knew that it was some bullshit about to come out of her mouth.

"Paul, I'm three months pregnant with your baby and I'm keeping it," she informed him, almost knocking the wind out of him.

"Say what?" He frowned.

Don spoke up for his daughter. "She's pregnant with my grandchild and she's keeping the baby is what she said."

"No disrespect to you, Mr. Don, but how do I know that this baby is mine? Am I your only sex partner, Melissa?"

"See what I'm saying, Daddy! I knew he was going to do this! This is why I wanted to have this conversation in front of you! He doesn't want me to have my baby because it's going to break up his happy home with that bitch, Vix."

"Answer his question, Melissa. He deserves to know that much."

"Yes! Absolutely! He is the *only* man that I've been sleeping with for the last six months," she stated truthfully.

"Fuck, man!" Paul stood up and kicked the chair.

"She's going to allow you to tell your wife, Paul. But my grandchild doesn't deserve to be a secret," Don said, trying to be understanding of Paul's situation as much as possible.

Melissa could do no wrong in Don's eyes. And whatever she wanted, she got.

Paul went for the door. "Alright, man. Just let me figure some shit out."

Melissa grabbed her purse and stormed out.

"*Fuck*!" Paul yelled when he walked outside.

Chapter Fifteen

Carstin's day couldn't get any better than it had been. Everything was going perfect at his store, he and Purity's relationship was perfect in his eyes, and the double date at his mother's house had turned out good. Claudia had gone in on the dinner like it was Thanksgiving. Purity was impressed that the day had turned out so perfectly. She knew that she had lucked up with Carstin and she couldn't thank God enough. She could only remember the days that her grandmother had told her to be patient, and that God was going to send her someone good. She was a firm believer at that point.

He and his stepfather, Richard, were in the kitchen throwing back a few Coronas, catching up while Claudia and Purity sat in the living room and ate cake.

"Got yourself a good one, huh?" Richard asked Carstin.

He smirked. "Yeah. A real good one."

Richard leaned in. "You hitting that?" he whispered.

Carstin laughed. "Chill out, old man."

"I'm just asking. Hell, the way you said that had me curious."

"She's different, but I like her ass a lot. I was her first in bed."

"Yeah, and you were that little girl, Erika's first too."

"I ran into Erika and her mama back in Baton Rouge. She's down there for school."

"She ain't doing shit but following you."

"I can't do shit for her. She's pregnant, big and pregnant."

"Erika's pregnant?" Richard asked, surprised.

"Same shit I asked. But yeah, she is."

The doorbell rang and Richard left Carstin in the kitchen to answer the door. They weren't expecting any visitors, but they had a lot of family who didn't mind popping up when they got ready.

"I'll get it, baby." Richard walked to the door with his beer in his hand. "Who is it?!" he yelled.

"It's Brenda." He frowned and opened the door, "Good evening," he greeted her.

"Hey, Richard. Is your wife home?" Brenda asked.

"Yes. Come on in."

The two of them walked into the living room and Brenda's unexpected visit took Purity and Claudia by surprise. Purity remembered her face from the restaurant when she and Carstin ran into Erika back at home.

Claudia stood to her feet and smiled, "Hey, Brenda. What brought you by?"

When Carstin heard her name from the kitchen he almost choked on his beer. He quickly made his way to the living room to join everyone.

"My daughter should be doing this, and it really isn't my place. But she's never going to do it herself." She cleared her throat. "Erika is now six months pregnant with Carstin's baby."

"What?!" Claudia, Carstin, and Richard yelled in unison.

"Yes. I begged her to tell Carstin when we ran into him in Baton Rouge, but she said that she wanted to do it herself. My grandbaby will be born in three months and Carstin needs to know this."

Carstin was so caught off guard he couldn't speak. All he could do was look into Purity's hurtful eyes.

The pain in Purity's chest made her think about the heartbreak she had when her grandmother died. She never wanted to experience that feeling again, but there she was.

"Hell nah! Y'all got me fucked up!" Carstin yelled.

"Damn sure do!" Richard agreed.

"Wait. Everyone, calm down for a second. Let me wrap my mind around this. So you're telling me that your daughter is pregnant by Carstin?"

"That's *exactly* what I'm saying."

"It ain't mine. How y'all wait until three months before the baby is expected to come and tell me some shit like that? And where's Erika? Why didn't *she* tell me?" Carstin argued.

"Carstin Anthony, watch your tone!" Claudia pushed him. "Now whether you like any of this or not, you are talking to a woman who is old enough to be your mother. You *will* respect her. Do you understand me?"

He nodded his head.

"I feel the same damn way, shit. How the hell she just gon' pop up and say some shit like that, Claude? Hell no. They're trying to set my boy up!" Richard fumed.

Purity put her shoes on and walked to the back of the house.

"See, this is exactly why I always told Erika she was wrong about you. You were never for my daughter, Carstin." Brenda shook her head. "My daughter was fine until she met you. Now she's pregnant, is probably going to be a single mom, and you want to dog her like she was a hoe. My baby was a virgin until she met you."

"Hold on now. Let's stop right there, Brenda. Now Carstin is *my* son, and he won't be disrespected. You come into my home and tell us that your daughter is six months pregnant with his child, but he has every right to be skeptical about this. If that's Carstin's baby, you don't have to worry about her being a single mother because the same way you raised Erika right, I raised my son right. But as far as him having a baby on the way, I won't go for it and he won't either. Not until we get a DNA test."

Brenda pulled out her phone and dialed Erika's number and put it on speaker.

"Hey, Mama," Erika spoke into the phone.

"I'm here at Carstin's mama house and I told them since you don't want to be a grown woman and do it. You're on speaker. Tell them, Erika. Tell them that this is Carstin's baby."

"Mama, you did what?" Erika yelled.

"Can I speak with her, please?" Carstin asked.

She handed him the phone.

"Come on, Erika! This is me! Why is your mama saying you're pregnant with my baby?" he asked her.

She cried into the phone and told him everything. In just five minutes he learned that she was six months pregnant with a little girl and she even told him the night he got her pregnant. He wanted to believe that it was his baby, but he just didn't know if the baby was his or not.

"Can I meet with you when I get back home tomorrow?" He looked at her mother and frowned. "Just you and me, though?"

"That's cool. Just call me whenever you're ready to meet."

He hung up the phone without saying goodbye.

"You can leave now. Thank you for stopping by." Richard showed Brenda to the door.

When Brenda got into her car she smiled. If they thought her baby was going to be the only one living in hell they had another thing coming.

Carstin walked into the guest room only to find Purity curled in the bed crying her eyes out. He dropped his head and shook it.

How the fuck can my life go from sugar to shit in less than twenty four hours? He thought to himself.

"Baby," he called out.

"Carstin, don't come anywhere near me. For real," Purity cried.

"Purity, I swear on everything I love, I didn't know," he swore.

"You're a liar!" she got out the bed and walked into his face. "I asked you when we saw that girl at the fucking restaurant if you had anything to tell, me and you lied to me. You knew, didn't you?"

"I didn't fucking know. What type of nigga you think I am, P? You think if I knew I had a baby, I would be hiding my fucking child? I didn't know and I put that on my mama."

Purity wiped her eyes and grabbed her phone.

"I'm catching a flight home. You don't have to worry about taking me back."

He snatched her phone. "No the fuck you're not."

She sat on the bed and broke down. "You promised not to hurt me, Carstin."Getting on his knees between her thighs, he looked her straight in the eyes. "I won't hurt you, bae. I won't. I don't even know if the baby is mine. I didn't know she was supposed to be pregnant by me, Purity."

"I just want to go home," she cried.

"Nah. We gonna go to my house and sleep this shit off. You and I both know I wouldn't do you like that, right?"

She shook her head."I *thought* I knew."

"You're tripping, man." He stood to his feet and paced the floor.

He had so much shit going through his head that it was crazy. If Erika was pregnant with his baby, he knew for a fact that Purity wasn't going to fuck with him, and that's not what he wanted. He had finally found the girl that he wanted to spend the rest of his life with, and the bullshit just had to follow him. He thought about what Erika had said on the phone and he was confused. It was true that when they were together he never used protection because he was the only person that she was sexually active with, but it was hard to believe. If she would've told him when she first found out it would've been easier to believe that it was his baby, but the fact that she kept it a secret for so long made him feel like she was trying to shit him.

"Could it be your baby?" Purity finally asked.

"I don't know, P. I mean we had unprotected sex a lot, so it could be my child. But the fact that she waited so long to tell me is what's making me feel like she's on the bullshit."

She began to cry again. "This isn't how it's supposed to be."

"I know. It wasn't my intention for it to be like this. You can't give up on me, though, okay?"

When she didn't respond, he shook her. "P?"

"Huh?" she snapped out of her trance.

"We're in this together, right?"

"I just don't have time for the baby mama drama, Carstin. I'm not built for all that drama. That's not me. I can see just from her mama that it's going to be a lot of shit, and I'm not for it. Then all this shit happens when everything is going good for us." She wiped her final tear.

"That's why you can't give up on me now. Even if this baby is mine, it won't stop what we got going on. It won't stop us from having our own family. This situation won't stop shit."

"We'll see how all this goes. Right now I just want to get some sleep."

"Okay. Come on." He handed her, her cell phone.

She sent Vanity and Vix a quick text message.

Purity: This nigga probably got a baby OTW! I want my virginity back! ☹

***

Carstin walked into Yogurt Land and stood in the middle of the building in search of Erika. He and Purity had made it back to Baton Rouge just a few hours earlier, and he was dying to sit down and talk with Erika. He needed to know what the hell was going on. She agreed to meet him there, but he didn't see her. Right when he took his phone out to call her, he saw her waving her hand in the air. He walked over to the table and took a seat across from her.

"What's up, Erika?" he greeted.

"Hey, Carstin. I'm sorry about all of this," she apologized.

He took a look at her and she was indeed pregnant. She was so beautiful and the pregnancy glow added to her beauty. He had to admit that she looked good.

"Is this my baby?" He got straight to the point.

She wiped the tears falling from her eyes.

"Yes. I'm so sorry that I didn't tell you in the beginning. We had just broken up, and I didn't want you to think that I was trying to trap you."

He wanted to drop his head, but he didn't want to offend her. It wasn't a secret that he didn't want to have a baby with her, but it seemed like that's what it was. Even though he still wanted a blood test, he knew she wasn't lying to him. He looked her directly in her eyes and he knew that she was telling the truth. Erika wasn't a bad girl and she had never lied to him. Carstin just hated that she had allowed her mama to rule her like she was a little ass girl.

"Damn, man, I'm not even being funny when I say this, Erika…but to be on the safe side, I would like a DNA test when the baby is born."

She nodded and began to eat her yogurt. "That's fine."

"Is that why you came to Baton Rouge?"

"No, I came here for school. I didn't even know I was going to run into you. I'm not trying to be the baby mama from hell. If my mama would've never come to your mama's house, I probably wouldn't have told you. I just want this to be peaceful."

"If this is my baby, and you would've kept her from me, I would've had a problem with that, but we'll get past that."

"Where's your girlfriend?" She licked her spoon.

"She didn't want to come. She wanted us to have this private time."

"You invited her?" She frowned.

"Hell yeah. What do you mean? That's my girl, and if this is my baby, she's going to be with me every time I need her to be. Is that going to be a problem?"

Erika wanted to tell him it would be a problem, but she had to remind herself that she wasn't with Carstin anymore. She wished like hell she was, though. She admired him in so many ways. When they were together he was faithful, open, and very committed to their relationship. If she could've changed the way she'd handled herself and her parents, she would've.

He looked so good sitting there with his arms crossed like a boss. His hair cut was fresh and lined up to perfection. His beautiful, thick eyebrows would make any woman jealous. He was still the laidback guy she'd fallen in love with back then. He rocked his white t-shirt, black baller shorts, and retro Jordan's so well.

She handed him a file. "I brought you something."

He opened it and almost choked up. She had a copy of each ultrasound from her doctor's visits in the folder, and Carstin wanted to shed a tear. He wasn't expecting for it to be like that.

"She's a healthy baby. She doesn't give me any problems at all. I'm just hungry all the time," she told him.

"Damn, man. A little girl, huh?"

"Yes." She smiled and nodded.

"What are you going to name her?"

"I want to name her Carlisa."

He shook his head. "That's ghetto as fuck."

"What do *you* want to name her?"

"Let me think of something. I don't like Carlisa, though."

"Are you going to have your girlfriend help you with a name?"

"Her name is Purity, Erika. And yeah, I might have her help me."

"You really love her?"

Erika couldn't act like she wasn't bothered. For so long she was the only girl that Carstin loved. There was no way in hell Purity had come along and made him change his mind that fast.

"Yeah, a nigga's in love. I won't lie about that. You and I just need to focus on the baby. That's all I want, Erika. I've already made up my mind about P, and she ain't going nowhere any time soon."

She threw her hands up in surrender. "Okay. Don't beat me up."

"Nah. I'm being straight forward with you since you won't be straight up with me. Say what's on your mind and don't beat around the bush."

Her eyes watered. "You moved on so fast. We could've worked it out."

"Your mama fucked that up, and you allowed it, so hey…" He shrugged. "We just didn't work out."

"Let's try it again, Carstin. I can do better."

"Nah, man. Don't make this hard, Erika. Let's handle this right."

"Okay." She wiped her tears away.

He reached over and rubbed her hand.

"Friends?"

"Friends." She smiled and shook his hand.

He reached in his pocket and gave her the stack of money that he had planned on giving her. It was a little over five thousand. "I'ma go shopping for her sometime this week, but take this and get the things you need. Okay?"

"Okay. Thank you."

They shared a hug and he left.

As soon as he pulled off from her, he called his big brother.

"What's up, little nigga?" Paul answered.

"Shit so fucked up, bruh. Remember my ex, Erika?"

"Yeah. What about her?"

"She's pregnant, and the baby is supposed to be mine."

"No shit?"

"Yeah, man. And she's still in love with a nigga. I had to make her ass shake on being friends."

Paul fell over laughing. Paul shook his head. "I'm in a fucked up situation myself."

"What's going on with you?" Carstin asked.

"Melissa's pregnant, and she's keeping the baby."

"What the fuck? Again?"

"Again, man. I can't lose my wife," Paul said, sadly.

"Damn, man. You gon' tell her?"

"Soon my nigga, soon."

"Let's link up later and go have some drinks or some shit."

"That's a bet, man."

He hung up and drove to Chrystal's house to go and tell Purity about his visit with Erika. Before he left she was in a good mood, but he prayed that it would stay that way after he gave her the news.

Chapter Sixteen

Vix bit down on her bottom lip and tried to keep from spazzing out on Paul as she scrolled through his and Melissa's conversation in his phone. The stupid nigga wasn't even smart enough to delete everything before he got into the shower. She now knew that Melissa was pregnant with his baby and they had been messing around a little over six months. Vix felt played. The entire time she was beating herself up about sleeping with Hazel, Paul was cheating on her with the same bitch had who had caused problems in their marriage. She had to play it cool, though.

She had gone looking for evidence and she'd found it. She was glad that she wasn't tripping when she thought he was up to no good. Instead of killing him like she should've, she was going to play it cool. Hazel was taking her, Vanity, and Vix to the Dominican Republican for a week vacation while Paul was going to Jamaica, and she couldn't wait until Paul left. By the time he came back, the house was going to be empty with no sign of her or their children.

"Bae, you saw that Gucci tie that I had laying on the dresser?" Paul asked.

She threw the phone on the other side of the bed before he could see her going through it.

"No, I didn't," her voice cracked. *Don't cry, Vix,* she said in her head. "What's the matter, bae? You need some more of this?" He held his hard wood and pushed up on her.

"No. I'm okay. You want me to take you to the airport?" She smiled.

"See, man, that's what I'm talking about. You're finally being nice to a nigga again." He kissed her cheek. "Yeah. You can drop me off. I'ma stay in Jamaica until Sunday. Ain't that when y'all come back from the girls' trip?"

"Yes, it is," she said calmly, watching him rushing to get his things together.

Once he was packed and ready to go, Vix drove him to the airport, blasting Usher's song, "Throwback."

"You remember when you came home? This used to be your favorite song."

"Yeah, a nigga had to do some of everything to win your heart. I'm so glad we're good now, man. Just thinking that our marriage was over had a nigga sick behind them bars."

She chuckled. "Boy, I tell you. You hurt me so bad back then. I still can't believe we bounced back from that shit." She shook her head and pulled into the airport.

He looked over to her and asked. "You alright?"

"Yes. I'm fine, bae. Give me a kiss before you leave."

He kissed her with so much passion.

Once he had all of his luggage out of the car and closed the door, Vix chuckled. "That's the last fucking kiss you'll ever get from me." She laughed and pulled off.

Paul didn't even know that he had awakened a sleeping beast. What pissed Vix off the most was that he had tried so hard to play on her intelligence, but she knew better. She knew that he had some sneaky shit up his sleeve.

She dialed Hazel's number, and he answered on the third ring.

"What's up, baby girl?" he asked.

"I'm all yours, babe," she cried.

Hazel could hear her sniffling. "What the fuck is wrong with you, Vix?"

"I knew I wasn't tripping. He's been cheating this whole time, and Melissa is pregnant." She broke down.

"Damn! For real? How long they been fucking around?"

"About seven months." She gripped the steering wheel tight out of frustration.

"Damn, baby. I'm sorry to hear that. What's your plan?"

"Can we come back two days early from our trip? I need to get everything from the house. I'll move in with you. I'll have divorce papers for that nigga sitting on the table for him when he comes back."

"Whatever you want to do is fine with me."

"Okay. I'm about to go finish packing my bags for the trip. The girls and I will be over there later tonight."

"Okay."

"Wait. Hazel?"

"Yeah?"

"I love you."

He smiled. "I love you too, Vix."

***

Vanity ate her cereal while she enjoyed a foot massage from Juice. He was so proud of her. She was now four months pregnant with his baby and she was excelling in school. He loved that she didn't allow the baby and her laziness to affect her school work.

"You need to go get a pedicure, Vanity. Your feet are rough as fuck at the bottom," Juice complained.

"I'll make an appointment in the morning when we get to the Dominican Republican. Can you go make me another bowl of cereal?"

"What the fuck? Hell nah. You just had three bowls."

"But my baby is hungry." She rubbed her belly, making Juice laugh.

"No the fuck it ain't. Don't blame that on my baby."

He took her bowl and fixed her more cereal.

Vanity was pissed when she heard her front door open until she saw Tarvis walk in with Sheika.

Juice frowned. "What the fuck you doing with Tarvis, Sheika?"

Sheika rolled her neck. "Boy, I'm grown."

"Yeah and you got some fucking nerve to be asking her some shit like that when you in here laid up with my little sister."

"This different, nigga. This my baby mama."

Tarvis balled his fist. "Yeah, your baby mama…but don't forget you got her pregnant behind my back."

"Okay, cut it out. This is getting old. For real." Vanity stood to her feet.

"This a *get back* thing?" Juice pointed to the both of them.

"Nigga, me and Sheika just been chilling. Unlike you, I don't fuck my best friend's sister behind his back."

"Y'all chilling *now*, but chilling turns into fucking." He sat down at the dining room table.

"You know about that, huh?" Sheika asked, peeling a banana.

"What's up, big girl? Let's leave them in here so they can talk in peace."

"I agree." Vanity walked off and stopped in her tracks to open the door. She knew that Vix would be coming by because she was the slow one out the group.

She opened the door and almost shitted on herself when she saw Crip standing there with food from the Waffle House in his hand. She had totally forgotten she'd asked him to bring her something to eat before Juice popped up.

Crip was the guy from the club that Tarvis and Juice told her was dangerous. Even though Juice had proven that he was faithful to her, she still didn't trust his word for some reason so whenever she had the free time, she and Crip would chill. He was nice, laidback, and sexy. They had never had sex, but he did give her head a few times and it was magnificent.

"You have to go," she whispered.

She was too late because Juice had already walked up behind her. When she saw the smirk on Crip's face, she turned around and looked at an angry Juice.

"Juice, he—"

He pushed her into the wall and punched Crip. Crip and the food went flying down the stairs. Juice ran down the stairs and punched Crip repeatedly in the face.

"You fucking with my baby mama, nigga?" He punched him.

"Juice, stop it! Stop it! It's not what you think!" Vanity yelled from upstairs.

When Tarvis heard the chaos, he ran outside and instead of stopping the situation, they double teamed him. They were passing him back and forth with blows like a hot potato.

Finally, Sheika and Vanity ran down to break them up.

"Chill before y'all get this fucking girl put out!" Sheika yelled.

"Fuck that, nigga!" Juice stepped back.

When he locked eyes with Vanity, she knew to run for her life—and she did. She tried to close the door, but she didn't succeed. He grabbed her around her neck and pushed her into the couch. He would've put his knee in her stomach to stop her from moving but he remembered she was pregnant.

"You've been fucking with this nigga while you pregnant with my seed?" He bit his lip and choked her harder.

"Nigga, are you crazy? Get the fuck off of her!" Tarvis pushed him to the floor.

"Y'all some crazy motherfuckers. Tarvis take me home." Sheika walked back into the house.

"You been fucking this nigga while you pregnant with my baby, Vanity?" Juice asked. He was so hurt and everyone in the room knew that.

She cried and caressed her neck. "I didn't have sex with him, Juice. We're just friends."

"*Just friends*? What the fuck did I tell you about that nigga, Vanity?" Tarvis yelled at her.

"He's dangerous," she said.

"So why can't you fucking listen?" Tarvis shook her.

He was convinced that Vanity was crazy. She didn't know how dangerous the nigga was and she didn't even know that he was after her for a reason and it wasn't because she was beautiful with a banging body. He and his niggas had been trying to kill Juice for years. The only thing that had protected them was their association with Paul's empire.

"And just to think a nigga tried to tie your hoe-ass down. You got me fucked up. A bitch will *never* make me look like a fool." Juice went off and stormed out of the house.

"Juice, wait." She ran down the stairs and grabbed his shirt. "I'm sorry. I'm so sorry. It's not what you think. I swear!" she cried.

"You know what, Vanity? I should've listened to what all the niggas said about you. You don't know shit about being a girlfriend. You just a fucking hoe and can't help that shit. And to think that we had been having marriage conversations. I'll be the dumbest nigga on earth to settle down with your fat ass. You don't even got enough class to not fuck with a nigga while you're pregnant with *my* child. And don't tell me you ain't fuck him because all you do is fuck niggas. If it ain't 'bout my baby, don't call me for shit. And that's real."

Sheika's mouth dropped open, and Vanity's heart stopped. She had never been disrespected like that before in her life and she was heartbroken. Sheika felt bad for Vanity, but Tarvis sure as hell didn't. He had always told her that her little nasty ways would catch up with her, and that's exactly what had happened. He was told to stay out of their relationship and that's exactly what he was going to do.

She looked back at Tarvis for a response, but he threw his hands up.

"I warned you about all of this," he told her.

She stormed back inside the house and slammed her door. She broke down and cried and dialed Vix's number. She could've screamed when she got her voicemail over and over. She knew for a fact she wasn't going to be able to go on the trip in the state she was in.

***

Purity let out a sigh of frustration. She and Chrystal had joined Tawny for her chemotherapy, and of course Tawny's disrespect was at an all-time high. She was being so rude and nasty to the nurses. It was ridiculous.

"Ma'am, we're going to need you to calm down. We go through this with you all the time," the nurse told her.

"I don't like the way that last bitch stuck that needle in my arm. I'm telling you now not to send her back in her. I'll knock her fucking head clean off."

"Tawny!" Chrystal called out. She was so embarrassed.

"I'm serious, Chrystal. You saw how she yanked my arm."

"I did catch that, but calm down, okay? I'll talk to your doctor about it." Chrystal rubbed her sister's hand. She knew that the only reason Chrystal was going off was because she was embarrassed about her health.

"She probably yanked it because you're so mean," Purity mumbled.

"Say it out loud, Purity. Don't mumble," Tawny said.

"It's a shame that even on your sick bed you're so mean and nasty to people, Tawny. I mean dang, can you be nice for once in your life?" Purity asked.

"Thank you," the nurse mumbled.

"You can get your ass out of here too. Send me somebody else!" Tawny snapped.

As mad as Chrystal was, she could only laugh. She had learned that all Tawny needed was a little attention, and she was going to be the one to give it to her.

Purity was so stressed out. Between work and Carstin, she didn't know what was killing her the most. Due to her two-week vacation, she was so backed up with work. She wanted to cancel on Vix's trip so bad, but she really wanted it. The fact that

Carstin was happy about the baby now drove her insane. She wasn't mad that he had stepped up to the plate and accepted the baby, but what about her? She was still the spotlight in his life, but it seemed so weird. Even though she tried to space herself away from him, he wasn't letting up.

"Aren't you supposed to be over Vix's house getting prepared to leave?" Chrystal asked.

"Yes, ma'am." She nodded.

"Where are y'all going?" Tawny asked.

"Dominican Republican. You want to come?" she asked sarcastically.

"Don't be funny, Purity."

Purity laughed. "I was just playing. I do have to get going though. Are you going to be alright?"

"I'll be fine. Chrystal is going to be here with me."

"Okay. Well, I love y'all. I'ma head over here to Vix's house. We leave in about two hours."

"Love you too!" Tawny yelled, which surprised the hell out of Purity.

Purity drove over to Vix's house in complete silence while her phone continuously rang. She didn't want to be a bitch towards Carstin but she was so hurt behind everything that went down with them in so little time. She just needed time to herself and maybe the trip would give her a peace at mind.

She knocked on Vix's door and was surprised when she turned the knob the door was open. When she heard Vix screaming and crying she dropped her purse and ran upstairs.

She found Vix on the floor cutting up her wedding pictures out of her album.

"Cousin, what's wrong?" Purity asked her.

"This nigga has been cheating on me the whole time, P. *The whole time*!" she screamed.

"How do you know?"

"I went through his phone. That bitch is pregnant."

"Are you serious?" Purity held her chest.

"Yes, but it's all good because I'm pregnant too and it ain't his fucking baby."

"You're what?"

"I'm pregnant with Hazel's baby. This whole time I've been beating myself up about stepping out on him, this nigga has been cheating. He's got me fucked up."

"What are you going to do?"

"I'm leaving his ass. He's gone to Jamaica. When we comes back from this trip, I'm packing my shit up and going right over there with Hazel. He'll have divorce papers waiting for him."

"Wow. I can't believe any of this shit."

When Vanity walked in the room with red, puffy eyes, Purity looked from the both of them.

"Okay, Vanity why you crying?"

"I fucked up y'all. Juice found out about me and Crip and he's done," she cried.

Purity thought she was going through some shit, but her cousins had it bad. She felt bad for the both of them, but she felt bad for Vixtoo.

"Does Paul know you're pregnant?" Purity asked.

"Pregnant? Wait. I'm so sorry, Vix. I came in here and took over. What's going on with you?"

"Paul is cheating," Purity spoke up for her.

"But so are you so don't that make it even?" Vanity asked.

"Nah he's been cheating on me for seven months, and the bitch is pregnant."

"*What!*" Vanity yelled.

"But I'm pregnant with Hazel's baby."

A sharp pain shot threw Vanity's head.

"Is all this shit really happening right now?" she asked.

Purity laid back on the floor. "Yeah, it is."

"I'm leaving Paul for Hazel. That's all there is to it. I'm not even in love with Paul anymore. I think I'm just more so hurt that he's been playing me for so long and I didn't even know it."

"I feel you, sis," Vanity sighed. "Juice is done with me." She wiped her tears. "He talked to me like I was the biggest whore ever."

The three of the ladies sat in the middle of Vix's bedroom floor and cried out their problems. All of them were hurting in their own way.

Chapter Seventeen

Melissa lay at the top of the bed while Paul was at the bottom texting and calling his wife. When she didn't answer he grew frustrated.

"What the fuck could she possibly be doing?" He threw the phone in the chair next to him.

"She's cheating on you," Melissa spoke up.

"What?" He turned around and frowned. "That's the last thing I'm worried about. Tell me something though, Melissa. Why you always worried about my wife? How come you talk about her like she done something to you? You're the one sleeping with a married nigga. Not her."

Melissa kicked the covers off of her and walked over to her purse.

"No, nigga. You should be worried because that bitch ain't worried about your ass. Every chance she gets she's fucking her ex, Hazel. And guess what? The joke is on you. See, while I've been patiently waiting on your dumb ass to come to your right senses and realize that I'm the one that you should be with, you just don't get it."

"Prove that she's been cheating, bitch. If you can't prove it, shut the fuck up. Bashing her to me won't make me be with you. I'm still wondering if you're pregnant with my baby."

She slung the file of pictures she had been taking of Vix in his face. "There's the proof right there, dumb ass."

When Paul flicked through the pictures he became furious. Melissa had been taking pictures of Vix every time she was with Hazel. She even had pictures of Vix leaving the doctor. After paying a lady behind a desk three thousand dollars, Melissa had learned that Vix was indeed pregnant and she would bet any amount of money that the baby wasn't Paul's.

Melissa laughed. "Cat got your tongue?"

He stood to his feet and put on his clothes.

"Shit, I guess she and I can call this shit even," he shrugged.

Melissa's eyes almost popped out of her head.

"You're going to stay with that bitch after this?" Melissa eyes watered.

"Yep and guess what? The joke's on you. You went out your way to prove something about my wife and that only made me love her more. Oh and no worries, Mama. I'll tell her about the baby you're carrying as soon as I get back home. As far as this connection I got with your daddy is concerned, consider that shit canceled. Now since I can come clean to my wife about your tired, hoe ass, I don't have to stay connected with y'all crazy motherfuckers to cover this shit up. I'm out."

He grabbed his packed bag, and slammed the door on his way out. It was only one thing on his mind and that was killing Hazel *and* Vix.

He called her and she didn't answer so he sent her a text.

Paul: You think you slick, but I got a trick for your ass.

***

Vix did everything she promised to do. When they got back in town from their wonderful trip, the girls helped her pack up the entire house. She took everything that belonged to her and her boys and had it moved to Hazel's house. She left a long unapologetic goodbye letter along with divorce papers on her old dining room table and left the house. Paul had been sending her texts threatening to kill her when he got back, but she was unbothered. She felt so safe being with Hazel and that's all that mattered to her.

As always, Hazel didn't give a fuck about Paul, and he was relieved that Vix had opened her eyes and realized who she belonged to. He never hated on Paul; and he wasn't going to start, but he was glad that she had finally seen that she deserved more than he was giving her. He wasn't going to rush her but the second she said she was ready he was going to marry her.

She knew that she was making the right decision when Chrystal approved of her leaving Paul to be with Hazel. Usually, Chrystal would've told her daughter that she was moving too fast, but she always admired Hazel more than Paul and when she found out that Paul was cheating on her she was definitely down for the whole divorce and moving on.

Hazel sat in his man cave and blew a blunt of loud while Vix was downstairs preparing dinner. The boys were at her mother's house, and they wanted to enjoy that day together.

Vix blasted Rihanna's new album on her iHome speaker and danced around the kitchen. When Hazel walked in and did his goofy dance to the song, "Work" Vix took out her phone and recorded him.

"Show them what you working with, baby," she laughed.

"I ain't gonna do it to them, bae," he said, waving her off.

She reached her arms out and motioned her hands for him to come into her. He walked to her and gripped her waist and pecked her lips.

"I love you, princess." He kissed her cheek.

"I love you too. How are you feeling?" she asked him.

"I feel good as fuck. You here to stay. That's the only thing a nigga like me needs to feel good."

She smiled and kissed him again. "Oh yeah?" When Vix heard Paul's voice, she screamed to the top of her lungs. Before Hazel could turn around good, Paul placed two bullets right in the middle of his head, splattering blood all over Vix's face.

Vix screamed. Instead of running she dropped down with Hazel.

She shook him. "Hazel! Baby, wake up!"

Paul grabbed her by her hair and dragged her through the puddle of blood.

"You think you're slick, bitch?"

She kicked and screamed, "Get off of me!"

"And you're *crying* over this nigga?" He pointed the gun to her head. "I'll kill your ass right here with him. Shed another tear."

She silently cried and continuously wiped the tears from her face. She was scared out of her mind.

Paul looked back and shot Hazel three more times just to let her ass know that it was no coming back for that nigga. When she screamed and cried louder he turned to her and shot her twice in the chest.

"I told you to shut the fuck up! Crying over this nigga, and shit."

He stepped over her not even checking to see if she was still alive and left the house.

to be continued…

ABOUT THE AUTHOR: Hello Readers, I'm Author Johnazia Gray, and I'm from Tallahassee Florida. I enjoy writing Urban Fiction. I'm signed under Jessica Watkins Presents. I've been signed since February 2016. I appreciate all my readers and thanks so much for supporting.

If you would like to receive email alerts when new Urban Fiction and African-American Romance are released, text the keyword "JWP" to 22828!

Jessica Watkins Presents is currently accepting submissions for the following genres: Street Fiction, Urban Fiction, African American Romance, African American Women's Fiction, Multicultural/Interracial Romance, BWWM Romance, and Paranormal Romance. If you are interested in becoming a bestselling author and have a complete manuscript, send the genre, word count, a synopsis and the first three chapters to jwp.submissions@gmail.com!